The
Stillness
in You

First published 2022

Published under licence by Brown Dog Books and The Self-Publishing Partnership Ltd, 10b Greenway Farm, Bath Rd, Wick, nr. Bath BS30 5RL

www.selfpublishingpartnership.co.uk

ISBN printed book: 978-1-83952-509-4
ISBN e-book: 978-1-83952-510-0

Cover design by Kevin Rylands
Internal design by Andrew Easton

Printed and bound in the UK

This book is printed on FSC certified paper

The

Stillness

in You

Katharina
Unverricht

BROWN
DOG
BOOKS

To my family, for always being there, no matter what.

To Rob, for sitting with me in the darkness
when I couldn't see the light.

As soon as you trust yourself, you will know how to live
Johann Wolfgang von Goethe

The most courageous act is still to think for yourself, out loud
Coco Chanel

Prologue

It was a stormy day in April, the kind that whips the hair out of your face and leaves you feeling slightly winded, barely able to breathe. Rain clouds hung low in the sky, ready to burst, blocking out the weak sun and giving the air a distinct chill. It wasn't an unusual day for the time of year and yet it was unlike any other day.

It was unique, distinguished from the rest and it would always stand out as such in the years that followed.

That stormy, rainy, chilly day in April was the day I finally broke free.

Chapter 1

Grace

Grace looked out over the vast expanse of ocean before her. The tide was coming in and waves were rolling towards her at speed, whipped into a frenzy by the wind that was chasing them towards the land. Grace burrowed her face in her scarf that was wound around her neck, both for warmth and comfort, as her fingers gripped the railings she was standing behind, drops of rain interlacing with her hands. She reminded herself to take a deep breath and to focus on the sea, the immensity of the water that seemed to dwarf every concern, every worry and force them into perspective. The wind lifted strands of her hair and toyed with them playfully as thoughts raced through her head and a playback of images danced across her mind, unfolding the last twenty-four hours.

And suddenly Grace's heart beat faster and her breath came in short bursts as the realisation of what she had done hit her afresh. Grace, who from day one had pretty much always done as she was told. Grace, who tried to live up to other people's expectations no matter how high or unreasonable. Grace, who did what you were supposed to do, to follow the path of education, career, marriage, children. Grace, who had learned from a very early age that you put others' needs before your own, always polite, always accommodating, always eager to please. Grace, who never put a step out of line, who very rarely spoke up or allowed herself to disagree with the people around her. Reliable, dependable, quiet Grace had just, a mere twenty-four hours ago, walked away from her steady job, her four-bedroomed house that she felt nothing towards and her bossy 'albeit with good intentions that were almost always misplaced' boyfriend.

She had walked away from it all without so much as a backward glance.

*

Grace couldn't exactly tell when things started to go wrong. Her childhood was a mostly happy one, her parents strict but supportive, wanting the best for their daughter. They pushed her to achieve academically but also provided her with the opportunity for other pursuits, tennis, dancing, drama class. None of which were Grace's choice, none of which she particularly enjoyed or was any good at. But the thought of disappointing her parents or of failing in their eyes scared Grace and so she studied, danced, acted and played tennis and basked in the glow of her parents' pride, never questioning the niggling feeling that rarely left her side and in time became a firm fixture in her life. When her parents suggested for Grace to study accountancy, she agreed with their wishes, mainly because that was what she had always done but also because she saw the logic in it. Accountancy was needed within the world and her chances of getting a steady job seemed promising. As it turned out, Grace took to accounting and enjoyed the number crunching. It made sense to her. As for the rest of university life, she found it confusing and frightening at times. Grace had always been quiet and some of her classmates' behaviour was not only alien to her but seemed downright ludicrous. There were times though when Grace quietly admired what her fellow students got up to. They seemed brave and knew exactly who they were or wanted to be. Back then Grace didn't know who she was and thinking about it now, she still didn't. Perhaps that was one of the reasons why she had taken the drastic measure of quitting her life.

*

Grace sighed and eyed the clouds with trepidation. Her travel bag was by her feet, packed with the essentials, her handbag slung over her shoulder. Grace had packed in painful clarity, really looking at things and realising for the first time how little her surroundings seemed to resemble her. Paul, her boyfriend of five years, had picked most of the furniture and although Grace seemed to vaguely remember discussions taking place, she had gone along with what Paul wanted; after all, his happiness had been her priority. She shook her head as sadness spread through her. The rain drops started to increase and Grace thought her priority now should be to find somewhere to stay for the night. She hadn't thought this through, another unlike-Grace thing to do. She had simply packed and taken the first train to the seaside. A slow smile spread across her lips. *Crazy*, she thought. *Maybe*

I am having some sort of nervous breakdown rather than a lapse in judgement? But right now it didn't matter. Grabbing her travel bag, Grace turned away from the turbulent sea and headed towards the tourist information building.

*

'I'm sorry, love, but I doubt you'll find anywhere tonight.' The woman at the tourist information had kind eyes. She appeared to be in her mid-fifties and was kitted out in a pale blue blouse with a cardigan over the top. Her eyes were rimmed by glasses that were attached to a beaded chain and were scanning the various hotel and B&Bs within the area on her computer screen. Her name tag said Gladys.

'There must be somewhere,' Grace said anxiously. What was she supposed to do? Worst case scenario she could take the train to the next town but it was getting late and Grace didn't fancy travelling on her own at night-time. She might have walked away from her life but there were limits she wouldn't cross.

'It's always a good idea to book ahead,' Gladys remarked but there was no reproach in her voice. Nevertheless Grace blushed.

'It was a spur of the moment thing,' she muttered.

Gladys peered at her over her glasses. 'I see.'

Grace began fiddling with the strap of her handbag, anxiety mounting slowly. What had she done?

'You could always drive on to the next town which is a bit bigger and would have more options. I could ring ahead for you and book a room for you?'

Grace shook her head. 'I haven't got a car and I don't fancy travelling on my own at night.' She nodded towards the darkening sky outside the window. Gladys followed her gaze and sighed.

'Fair enough. Well the only other option I can suggest is that you stay at Josephine's place.'

'Josephine? Who is that?'

Gladys took off her glasses. 'Josephine is a local woman, has lived here pretty much forever. She owns a house up the hill and has two spare rooms that she lets out. Nothing official, mind you. It's more on a private basis, she doesn't even have a website, more word of mouth if you know what I mean?'

Grace blinked back at her. This sounded rather dubious. 'What is she like?'

Gladys chuckled. 'Josie is all right, she's one of a kind but she has a good heart underneath the prickly exterior.' Gladys took in Grace's pale face and look of terror and laughed. 'You'll be fine, love,' she reassured her. 'Now then,' she continued, 'I'll give her a quick ring.'

After several phone calls, Gladys tracked down Josephine, who didn't appear to have a mobile (really? in this day and age?), and after a brief conversation Gladys hung up.

'Right then, that's sorted. She has a room available and it's yours. You can sort the price and things with Josephine yourself.' Gladys smiled, satisfied that she had done her job.

Grace bit her lip. 'Ok, thank you,' she said. 'So how do I get to the house? Do you have an address?'

'Josephine is still in town, at the café. If you go there now, she can take you with her. Saves you walking.' Grace nodded. After saying goodbye to Gladys and thanking her for her help, she walked the short distance to the café. It had a pretty facade with big windows that advertised tea and cake paraphernalia and on the whole looked very inviting. Grace felt anxious. She would have preferred to stay in a hotel where staff would have been attentive and distant. She wanted to sink into soft pillows and let her mind wander. Then you should have booked ahead, she heard Gladys's voice. *Yes I should have*, she thought. With a sigh of resignation, she pushed open the door.

The café was pretty much empty and a woman was sweeping the floor. It was a big space with a counter at one end and mismatched tables and chairs arranged throughout. There was art on the walls and two giant blackboards behind the counter informed guests about the cakes and drinks on offer. Grace's stomach rumbled. She was starving. Looking around, she couldn't spot anyone.

'Excuse me?' she said to the woman sweeping the floor.

'Oh I'm sorry but we're closing,' the woman said apologetically.

'That's ok, I'm looking for Josephine? Gladys from the tourist information sent me.'

'Oh right, you must be Grace,' the woman replied. 'Nice to meet you, I'm Holly.' They shook hands. *At this rate, I'll be on first name basis with half the town before the night is over*, Grace thought.

'Josie is just over there,' Holly pointed to a dark corner. Grace narrowed her eyes and could make out a shape clutching a cream coloured mug.

'Thanks,' she said to Holly and walked over to where Josephine was sitting.

'Excuse me,' she said, 'are you Josephine? I'm Grace, Gladys from the tourist information sent me. I believe you said that I could rent one of your rooms?'

The woman looked up at Grace. She had blue eyes and a striking face with high cheekbones and although there were lines and wrinkles, they added to her character rather than ageing her. Her hair was white and gathered into a long, plaited braid that was slung over one shoulder. Her slender hands were wrapped around the mug that Grace could now see was coffee.

'Yes, hello, Grace, sit down.' It wasn't an invitation and Grace warily sank into the chair opposite. She could feel Josephine's eyes on her, mustering her.

'You look tired,' she stated.

Grace nodded. 'It's been a long day,' she replied.

'Gladys mentioned that you arrived here today but didn't book ahead. Now you can have the room as agreed, however, there are a few things we need to talk about first before I take you to my house.' Anxiety gnawed at Grace. All she wanted was a bed for the night but she nodded.

'Ok.'

'What brings you here?' Grace briefly considered making up some story but one look at Josephine's face and she thought better of it. She had an inkling this was not a woman to be messed with so she decided to tell her the truth.

'I quit my life.'

'You quit your life? How does one do that?'

Grace bristled. This was getting very personal, very quickly.

'With all due respect it's not any of your business, but the short version is that none of it felt right anymore and the only thing that did feel right was to leave.'

'Huh,' Josephine leaned back in her chair and regarded Grace thoughtfully. There was a moment's silence.

'All right,' Josephine said. 'The room costs forty pounds a night, which is non-negotiable. I don't run a B&B, it's more of a guest house, so you're responsible for your own meals, however, you can use the kitchen as long as you clean it up afterwards.'

Grace nodded.

'Excellent,' Josephine smiled. 'Now then let's get you back. Holly,' she hollered, 'get Grace here a coffee to go, please, she looks like she needs it.'

A few minutes later, they walked outside, the cool night air feeling like a welcome balm on Grace's tired skin. Josephine walked quite fast for an elderly lady, although Grace couldn't figure out quite how old she was and felt that at this stage it would probably be impolite to ask. Besides, she didn't want to risk losing the room. Josephine stopped in front of a cherry pink Mini Cooper. Grace's eyes widened in surprise.

'This is your car?' She had expected something more sensible or sedate looking.

Josephine chuckled, her eyes twinkling. 'I might be getting old, my dear, but I still know how to have fun.' Grace smiled. She had no idea where she was going or what lay ahead but she had no doubt that with Josephine by her side, it would be an interesting journey.

*

Grace woke up disorientated. This was definitely not her room. It smelt different. It felt different. Where was she? As she slowly opened her eyes, the previous day came rushing back to her. She had walked out of her life. She took a deep breath and as a her eyes adjusted to the dim morning light, she surveyed the room. She had felt too tired last night as Josephine had driven them back and had briefly shown her the downstairs before pushing a key into her hands. The room was pretty, if a little dated. Grace was currently lying in a comfortable double bed with a messing frame and a yellow and sage chequered blanket draped across her feet. *I must have slept the sleep of the dead,* she thought, as she normally tossed and turned and would have bet her right arm, if asked, that the blanket would have ended up in a heap on the floor.

There was a wooden wardrobe on one wall and a small pine desk with a chair in front of the window that was adorned with thick white curtains. The walls were painted a calming if faded yellow and there were a couple of framed landscapes adorning the walls. On her white painted bedside table stood a small lamp. *This could do with a bit of TLC,* Grace thought, who was used to the sleek lines of the modern furniture Paul had meticulously selected for their bedroom. At the thought of Paul her heart constricted and she reached for her phone. Grace had written him a letter trying to explain her reasons for what she felt she needed to do but knowing Paul he had probably only skimmed over it, thinking she had lost her mind. Maybe she had. The display showed a dozen missed calls and messages. Grace sighed. She had no desire to talk to Paul. Not yet.

Grace had met Paul at a work convention. He was good looking with brown hair and chocolate brown eyes. Grace had been attracted to him and as he struck up a conversation with her in the coffee break, she had found herself laughing at his jokes and had agreed on the spot to have dinner with him. And that was probably the last spontaneous thing she had done since then.

Until now.

Paul, it turned out, was brilliant at his job and a meticulous planner. Grace hadn't minded when he took charge of their relationship because he was kind and took care of her. And after all she was used to living life on other people's terms. She loved Paul, she still did, but God, she had been such an idiot. Is this what it felt like to have a breakdown? Breakdown or not, she needed to figure out who she was and what she wanted before it was too late. This much had become painfully obvious. And try as she might, she couldn't do that cooped up with Paul and working a cushy job. There was no room for reinvention. That was how she had felt and why she had decided on the spur of the moment to walk away.

She opened up a new message and her fingers flew over the keyboard with practised ease.

Paul, I'm fine. Don't worry. Read the letter! Grace x

She agonised for a moment over the kiss, then pressed send, and with a determination that startled her, turned off her phone.

Grace took a deep breath and felt relief flood her body. She swung her legs out of bed and padded over to the window, drawing aside a curtain to look outside. The house stood on a hill overlooking the town and the sea.

The rain that had started last night was still hanging in the misty air, dark clouds speckled the sky and the road below glistened like a black diamond. Grace might have just taken a giant, monumental, life changing step but the weather was indifferent, following its own rhythm, its own moods. Grace let go off the curtain and turned back towards the silent room.

Today was her first day of her new, own life. The gravity of that nearly floored her.

All right then, Grace, she thought to herself. *What now?*

*

In the end, Grace had decided to stick with some part of her routine, partly for comfort and partly because she really did not have a plan, but surely she would come up with one in time. The bathroom was located at the end of the hall and like everything else seemed pretty but dated. Grace switched on the shower over the bath and crossed her fingers for warm water. When the steam rose off the stream of water, Grace took it as a good sign and luxuriated for longer than usual, letting the water massage away the knots in her neck and shoulders. For an old house, the water pressure was surprisingly good. Half an hour later she was dressed in jeans and a knee-length cardigan and was entering the kitchen in search of a cup of coffee when her eyes met hazel brown ones and she came to an abrupt halt. There was a giant St Bernard's dog lying in front of the oven, watching her curiously. Grace didn't know anything about dogs. Was it friendly? Was it going to bite her? What should she do? The dog raised its eyebrows as if mocking her.

'Oh don't you mind Biscuit,' Josephine said as she swept into the kitchen from another doorway. 'He's not going to eat you, he's soft as anything really.' Josephine stroked the dog's head.

'Biscuit?' Grace asked. What an odd name for a dog.

Josephine chuckled. 'Well we had an incident when he was younger where he got into a cupboard and ate all the biscuits, hence the name. Suits him though, doesn't it? And who doesn't like biscuits?'

Grace couldn't argue with that.

'I was just going to make some coffee,' she said. 'Would you like one?'

Josephine studied her and Grace shifted uncomfortably.

'Sure, I'll have a cup of coffee. Why don't you help yourself and come sit with me in the living room,' she nodded in the direction of the lounge. 'Come on, Biscuit,' she said as she left the room again. The dog obediently roused himself and threw Grace another glance before trotting after his mistress.

Oh, Grace, she thought. *What have you got yourself into?!*

*

A short while later, Grace sat in a comfy armchair adjacent to Josephine, nursing an excellent cup of coffee and letting her mind wander. Biscuit lay curled up on the rug, dosing, seemingly having lost all interest in Grace. *Story of my life,* she thought.

'So,' Josephine broke the silence. She was wearing jeans and a flower-printed long-sleeved top, her hair braided again and falling over one shoulder. 'Do you want to talk about what it's like to quit your life?'

Grace met Josephine's eyes. Despite her directness, there was kindness there. And after all she had saved Grace from sleeping on a park bench.

She sighed. 'It's a long story.'

'Sweetheart, I've got nothing but time.'

As do I, Grace thought. And so she began to talk.

It took Grace almost two hours to tell Josephine the full story and she had surprised herself by how much she had divulged. But Josephine radiated empathy and a quiet knowledge and understanding that things were rarely black and white. Grace had felt drained, emotionally spent and Josephine had suggested that she should take Biscuit for a walk. Grace had been doubtful. She knew absolutely nothing about dogs and Biscuit wasn't exactly small. Josephine had merely waved away her concerns and so she was walking along the seafront towards the beach, the large dog straining at the collar to get there, delight written all over his face. *At least it looks like delight*, Grace thought. Delight and a whole load of slobber.

As soon as her shoes hit the firm sand she unclipped Biscuit's lead and he raced off, leaving paw prints in the sand. Josephine had assured her that Biscuit was well trained so Grace took a chance. After all, wasn't she all about taking chances now?

She hadn't realised how cathartic it would be to say her thoughts out loud. She felt a sense of clarity and even though right now she didn't know what her next step would be, she knew that she had made the right decision. What a novel feeling!

Grace walked along the beach, letting the cool air wash over her. There was something intrinsically calming about being near the water, she thought. Maybe that's why Josephine lived here. She didn't know much about the older woman but their chat this morning had invited closeness and she hoped that she would get to know Josephine a bit better.

Biscuit had stopped some way in front and gazed back at her with kind, brown eyes. His face looked like he was smiling. Grace's lips curved into one of her own. Then he barked, a single loud bark as if to say, come on, what are you waiting for?! Grace's smile grew wider as hope filled her.

What indeed am I waiting for? she thought as she quickened her pace to catch up with Biscuit.

Chapter 2

Owen

The first day I saw Josephine Taylor my heart stopped beating for at least 10 seconds. It was one of those rare hot summer days in July, the kind everyone wishes for, but when one actually happens, all you hear is complaints about the stifling heat, sunburn and the fact that the bottled water in the supermarket is sold out. Even though before you know it the heat is replaced by cold winds and a bucket load of rain and everyone goes back to wishing for a good summer. Welcome to Britain!

During that particular summer I had been working down in Cornwall and decided to walk back to my temporary home. The sky was deep blue with not a cloud in sight and the sun still stood proudly, casting its warmth across the land. The sea was calm, waves gently lapping to shore where people sat chatting and eating ice cream, toddlers running excitedly towards the water's edge only to shriek with delight when a wave washed over their tiny feet.

I followed the walkway that led along the promenade towards the town centre and eventually my destination. And then I heard laughter, shrieking and pleas of 'You don't have to do this' that instantly sparked my curiosity and made me look up. And there she was, standing on the rocks that protruded out over the sea, a circle of what I assume were her friends around her.

'You're wrong,' she said, a small smile playing on her lips as she looked over the edge and assessed the drop. 'I totally have to do this.'

More cries and laughter from the bystanders. *She wants to jump,* I thought, looking at the drop myself from where I was standing. It was a good four metres and there was no doubt that there would be rocks hidden underneath the calm water. *Why would anyone want to do this?* I thought, unable to look away. I had stopped walking at this point, it seemed my feet were rooted to the spot. I was aware that a few other people had also stopped to watch what was happening.

The girl gathered up a flower-printed summer dress and in one quick move drew it over her head and tossed it aside. A slender body emerged, dressed in a swimming costume. The girl walked to the edge of the cliff, blond hair falling down her back. She's stunning, I thought, and then my heart stopped as she took a breath, raised her arms over her head and jumped. No hesitation, just one graceful movement. I watched as she flew towards the endless blue of the ocean, fearing the worst.

And then nothing.

Where was she? Did she need help? Should I go in? I glanced at her friends, who looked over the cliff top scanning the water. They didn't look too worried.

And then suddenly she broke through the surface, triumphantly, to the cheers of her friends, water droplets glittering in her hair like diamonds. I took a breath and my heart started beating again. I knew right then and there that

I was in trouble, that my life had irrevocably changed and would never be the same again.

Josephine Taylor is a force to be reckoned with and as it turned out she was all I ever wanted and all I ever needed.

Josephine (Josie) – Then

Josie had learned from an early age to be independent. Being the daughter and only child of two semi-professional artists who were short of time had seen to that. Her father was a talented violinist whereas her mother excelled at playing the piano in a way that left people awed and speechless. The fact that she also had a beautiful singing voice meant that people adored her even more.

Her parents toured a lot with the orchestra they were both part of, leaving Josie in the capable hands of her nanny, Mrs Winter. The pregnancy had not been planned but at the time adoption or abortion were not looked upon kindly and Josie's mother had continued with the pregnancy, not only because, in her eyes, it was the moral thing to do but also because she was married and people expected there to be children. That social box would be neatly ticked.

Her mother did not have an easy pregnancy and Josie remained an only child. She often wondered whether this was a blessing or a curse. She didn't dislike her parents; they were supporting and loving in their own way but she understood from an early age that music was her parents' first love. If she wanted comfort or attention it was Mrs Winter she went to.

Mrs Winter was a middle-aged woman with a stocky build and a kind face. She laughed more often than most people and always had a kind word up her sleeve. But she could be stern too when needed and Josie was pretty sure she drove Mrs Winter around the bend as she grew older, always determined to do her own thing and challenging the status quo.

Most of the things she now knew, how to bake the perfect Victoria sponge cake or planting herbs or growing fruit and vegetables from seed, she learned from Mrs Winter. Even the vital conversation about sex that gives most parents sleepless nights came from Mrs Winter.

'Now you listen carefully, Josie,' she had said one spring morning when Josie was sixteen years old. 'Your virginity is a gift. Choose carefully whom you give it to. And don't take any crap from those pretty boys.' At a time when sexual revolution was ripe, her words had seemed old fashioned, and yet they held a truth Josie wished she would have appreciated at the time.

Shortly after that conversation, her parents no longer saw the need for a nanny and Josie was mostly left to her own devices. When news reached them that Mrs Winter had died following a heart attack, she was devastated. Her parents had sent a large bouquet of flowers and their condolences but did not attend the funeral. It seemed a meagre offering considering all the heavy lifting Mrs Winter had done for her parents.

Josie couldn't wait to spread her wings. Whilst her parents were often absent, they did have expectations of her. They wanted her to have an education and a career.

And so it came that Josie was standing on that rock on

a glorious summer day, a last hurrah before venturing into the world of work. Her parents had paid for her to go to Cornwall with her friends for three weeks before she was expected to enrol on a bookkeeping course back home. The blue water beckoned her from below, promising a cool and refreshing reprise of the summer heat. Before she could think too much about it, Josie had stripped off her summer's dress and stood at the edge of the rock, taking a deep breath before jumping. And that was how she met Owen.

He was standing at the edge of the water as she broke the surface, tall, in workman's boots, green eyes twinkling at her, an amused smile on his lips.

Her friends were cheering from the rock above and Josie looked at them with a quick smile before returning her gaze to Owen. She emerged out of the water as gracefully as she could manage, trying to ignore the butterflies in her stomach at the sight of this handsome stranger.

'That was quite a tumble you took,' he said, laughter in his deep voice.

'I think you'll find I dived,' she replied, not breaking eye contact whilst wringing out her long hair.

'Deathwish?'

'More of a thirst for adventure.'

He laughed. 'I'm Owen,' he said and held out his hand.

'Josie,' she shook his hand, noticing its rough texture. Definitely workman's hands.

'Would you like to have a drink with me?' Nerves had crept into his voice.

'I'm afraid I'm not exactly dressed for drinks,' she replied, a smile on her lips.

'Right, of course,' Owen blustered. 'How about drinks and dinner later?'

It took Josie barely a moment to agree. She liked Owen. Not only was he handsome but he also seemed sure of himself, but not so sure that he took her answer as a given. They arranged a time and place. Josie saw her friends rushing towards her, her dress and a towel in hand. Owen made to leave.

'See you later,' he said. 'It could be an adventure.' That smile again.

Moments later Josie was surrounded by her friends, who were chatting excitedly. *I have a feeling the adventure has already begun,* she thought to herself as she watched Owen walk away.

*

Josephine smiled as she allowed herself to remember. Hearing Grace talk about her life and why she decided, perhaps temporarily, perhaps more permanently, to walk away had brought back memories of Josie's own youth. She so very rarely allowed herself to think back to that time. Owen had been a big part of her life but their time had been cut short, leaving her devastated and heartbroken, a shadow of her former self. She wasn't the same person and so her life couldn't be the same either. Josephine moved through the rooms in her house, absentmindedly touching an ornament or running a finger down the spine of a book. She was glad she had sent Grace and Biscuit for a walk. She felt strangely unsettled.

Back then, after there was no going back, she had boxed up her memories and shoved them at the very back of her mind, buried her feelings deep inside the darkest corner of her soul. Her fear had always been that if she opened the box, what was left of her would crumble into pieces.

Now she wondered if that was true. She had once been that fearless girl with a hunger for adventure and a yearning for love. Perhaps she recognised a kindred spirit in Grace, even though they were generations apart. Grace was a young, vibrant woman with a streak of stubbornness. Josie wondered whether those characteristics were still a part of her, buried somewhere within herself, or whether she had lost them forever. Time leaves her mark on all of us, she thought.

Owen. An image danced across her mind of him smiling at her. That smile that made her weak at the knees and turned her stomach to mush.

Perhaps it was time.

Grace

It didn't take long for Grace and Josephine to fall into a routine. Grace was naturally a thoughtful person, sometimes too thoughtful, a people pleaser at heart, and stepped in where ever she felt most useful. Besides, the daily chores, whilst perhaps mundane, distracted her from the magnitude of her recent decisions and the fallout that would no doubt reach her sooner or later.

Her mobile phone constantly buzzed with messages, calls

and notifications, and Grace felt hunted by the people in her life. She knew that they didn't understand why she had done what she did and how could they? Grace barely understood it herself. In the end she had turned off her phone and had shoved it at the back of the drawer in her bedside table. At least for now.

Grace and Josephine, or Josie, as she insisted Grace should call her; 'Only my mother called me Josephine in the most disapproving tone,' she had told her, shared their morning cup of coffee together before Grace took Biscuit out for his first of two walks every day.

Grace relished this time alone with only Biscuit, running ahead of her on the beach. She enjoyed the way her thoughts wandered from this to that and how the wind from the sea would rush at her, tearing at her hair. She felt like the wind was blasting away the cobwebs, invigorating her with energy, leaving behind a clear mind.

Other times, however, Grace found herself worrying. Worrying about money, about work, about her future, about what people were saying about her, she who never put a foot out of line, suddenly gone crazy and run away from home. Grace tried to push those worries aside, she wasn't ready to deal with any of it just yet.

Even though these thoughts and worries weighed her down, there were moments when Grace suddenly realised she had the freedom to shape her day the way she wanted to. There was nobody to tell her what to do, what to think, nobody else's needs to consider. The sensation was both gratifying and dizzying at the same time.

Occasionally, Grace would stop by the café she had visited

on her first night before heading back to the house. Biscuit would lie panting at her feet, whilst she sipped a cappuccino, soaking up the hustle and bustle around her. Grace had struck up an easy friendship with Holly, who owned the café, and they would often have a quick chat. Sometimes they would talk about Josie. Holly had grown up in the town and had known Josie for some time.

'She's lovely isn't she? Doesn't mince her words, mind you, but I've come to think that's a good thing. At least you know where you stand, don't you?'

Grace had nodded in agreement. 'I do have a feeling though that she keeps people at arm's length,' Grace remarked.

Holly had nodded. 'Yes she does. Josie is a very private person. She knows most things about most people but she doesn't give much away.'

The conversation had moved on to different things but Grace had mulled over this piece of information. After all she had pretty much served up her life on a silver platter whereas Josie had indeed offered very little in return. Then again, it wasn't tit for tat and perhaps in time Josie would feel comfortable with Grace to maybe share one or two things about her own life.

But Grace couldn't deny that she felt intrigued by Josie. She was so different from some of the older people Grace knew. Her grandmother would never have set foot in a Mini Cooper, never mind drive one and a bright pink one at that. Josie seemed to live her life on her own terms, by her own rules. Grace, on the other hand, had always followed the path laid out before her by first her parents, then Paul.

Of course there had been times when she had questioned things, she wasn't a mindless idiot after all, but in the end, the cost of challenging the status quo had always seemed too high, the conflict too overwhelming that in the end she had simply complied, thinking that the people around her were only looking out for her and maybe, just maybe, they did know best. Until it had all come crashing down.

Perhaps that was why Josie seemed so interesting to her. She defied conventions and yet she was well liked within the community, but even more so, she seemed to be at ease with herself, accepting rather than critical. And Grace began to look at her like a striking light in the darkened wilderness of her soul, illuminating a new way of being and Grace, who had just broken free from everything familiar, felt like she was being reborn, like she was seeing the world and most importantly herself with fresh eyes, readying herself to make her mark on an unsuspecting world.

Chapter 3

Josephine (Josie) – Now

Josie was mixing the batter for the sponge cake and enjoyed the sensation of putting some welly into her stirring. She couldn't remember the last time she fancied baking a cake but she thought that Grace might appreciate a slice of Victoria sponge cake with her afternoon coffee. Strange, she thought, she never considered baking a cake for any of her other guests, but then most people that stayed at her house only stayed for one or two nights and remained strangers, whereas Grace already seemed like a friend, even though she had only been with Josie for a short time. Beads of sweat formed on her forehead and Josie swiped them away with her hand.

'Do you need any help?' Grace asked as she walked into the kitchen.

'No, I'm ok, love, thank you.'

'Ohh this looks good,' Grace said appreciatively, peering into the bowl.

Josie smiled.

'That's a pretty necklace,' Grace said and pointed towards the turquoise ring that was threaded on a chain, dangling from Josie's neck. Usually Josie kept it hidden underneath her cardigans and sweaters but she was only wearing a t-shirt now. She tried hard to keep her voice steady.

'Thank you.'

'It's an unusual colour, where did you buy it?' Grace asked, curiosity written all over her face. She was only being kind, Josie thought, but her heartbeat accelerated. She hadn't spoken about Owen for such a long time.

'It was a present,' she replied carefully. 'From Owen.'

There was a silence.

'That's lovely. I hope you don't mind me asking, but who is Owen?'

'My boyfriend. A long time ago,' Josie replied after a moment. The understatement of the year, she thought quietly. 'Now then why don't you get the jam out of the fridge whilst I put this in the oven?' she said, hoping that she did not have to say anymore on the matter.

Grace, who had a feeling she had to tread carefully, smiled and nodded. After all, she knew when she was beaten.

Owen

I chose a fish restaurant I knew for our first date. It was the first thing that popped into my head. I nearly fell over in shock when she agreed to meet for a drink and dinner. I had fully expected her to tell me where to go but it just goes to show that sometimes it pays off to take a risk. After all what did I have to lose? Sure, my pride would have been bruised if she had rejected me but I would have lived.

Fisherman's was a local place with an excellent bar and

the best fish and chips for miles around. It was always packed and always loud but in a good, friendly way. Joe, the owner, made everyone feel welcome and was adept at creating a relaxing atmosphere, inviting people to linger over coffee or another drink or three.

I had spent the rest of the afternoon worrying about what to wear. I know that's very unmanly of me. After trying on pretty much everything in my wardrobe, I went with dark denim jeans and a blue and black chequered cotton shirt with the sleeves rolled up.

I waited nervously outside the restaurant before telling myself in a very manly fashion to get a grip. She'd agreed to come after all, hadn't she?!

A nerve-racking ten minutes later, I was beginning to think that she might have agreed to the date but she wasn't going to show. Well done, Owen, my not-so-manly inner voice mocked me.

'You sure look happy to see me.'

I spun around and there she was, looking stunning in a floaty summer dress.

'Hey, you came,' I greeted her, my throat suddenly dry.

'You weren't worried, were you?' She smiled.

'Only a little,' I admitted, before holding the door open. 'Shall we?' We stepped into the music and laughter.

'What kind of food do they do here?' she asked.

'Best fish and chips in the region. I promise you!' God, I sounded like an advert for the place, but Josie merely smiled and we followed a waiter to a table.

I don't know what it was, maybe the food or the wine, but Josie and I hit it off. We talked, laughed and talked some more. It was like we became the best versions of ourselves in this bubble of music and good food. I forgot to be nervous and the conversation flowed easily. Josie devoured the fish in a way I have never seen a woman eat. Hungrily, making appreciative noises with each forkful and she ate everything that was on her plate. She was not one of those girls I had been on dates with before, who ordered a salad with dressing on the side and then pushed it around the plate, taking a careful nibble every so often.

'Best fish and chips ever,' Josie declared. 'You were right!'

'No, not ever, just around here,' I corrected her.

She gave me a sceptical look.

'Are you being facetious?'

'No not at all, I would never dare,' I replied, placing a heart on my chest in mock horror and she laughed. God, that laugh. It was to become my favourite sound.

'The best fish and chips is to be found on the Isle of Mull.'

'Is that so?'

'Yes, ma'am.'

'And where is that?' she asked, reaching for her wine glass.

'Scotland.'

'Is that where you're from?'

'Can't you tell from my accent?' I teased her. I knew that it was faint due to all the time I've spent travelling and working abroad.

'Nobody likes a know it all, Owen,' she reprimanded me, but her eyes had a mischievous glint. Despite myself I laughed.

'Enough about me. Let's talk more about you.'

'What do you want to know?'

'Everything, Josie. I want to know everything about you.'

At this point I already knew with a certainty that I only rarely possess that I was falling for this girl. She was unlike any woman I had ever met and she had captured my heart from the moment I saw her jumping from that rock into the waves below.

Josephine (Josie) – Then

Two weeks after that initial dinner, they had not only become a couple but inseparable. Owen understood her in a way no one else did, not even her friends, kind and funny though they were. They fell in love, quickly, deeply, unapologetically.

Two months later Owen took her home to meet his family. And here Josie fell in a love all over again, this time with the Isle of Mull. Wild and beautiful with ever-changing weather, the island was everything Owen had described but it was also so much more. It touched Josie on a fundamental level, imprinting itself onto her soul. Owen took her on a day trip to Tobermory, a small picturesque seaside town where she did indeed have the best fish and chips. Ever!

Grace

Once the cake had been baked and they sat in the living room, a big slice and a cup of coffee in front of them, Grace decided to give it another try.

'This cake,' she said, 'is seriously to die for.'

Josephine smiled, delighted. 'I'm glad you like it,' she said. 'Owen's favourite,' she added after a pause.

It's now or never, Grace thought.

'How did you meet?' she asked, keeping her tone neutral.

Josie didn't reply for a long time.

'I was down in Cornwall, on holiday with my friends before starting a bookkeeping course. My parents were keen for me to have a career, you see. It was a hot summer and I decided to jump off this rock into the sea to cool down and Owen, well, he must have watched me jump because when I came out of the water, he was standing there, handsome as anything and he asked me out.'

Grace smiled. 'He sounds very decisive.'

'Decisive, yes,' Josie agreed, 'that's a good way to describe Owen.' Grace noticed that Josie was fiddling with her necklace absentmindedly.

'Did he live in Cornwall?' Grace asked.

Josephine shook her head. 'No, he was working there over the summer. Owen worked as a carpenter by trade and he travelled all over the place. Thinking back now, it was quite by chance that we met really. I have to admit that after our first date, I didn't see much more of my friends. We spent all our free time together.'

Josie smiled a dazzling smile and it wasn't hard for Grace to imagine what she must have been like as a young woman. Grace took another sip of coffee, waiting for Josie to continue talking but she remained silent.

'It sounds like it was love at first sight,' she said. Josie laughed.

'Isn't it always when you're young? But I have to admit we

were very much in love and became inseparable, much to the despair of my parents.'

'Why was that?'

'Because,' Josie answered, 'after meeting Owen, I had no intention of doing the bookkeeping course my parents were so keen for me to do. Not long after we met, Owen took me home to Scotland to meet his parents and I fell in love with the place. And we made plans to settle there, start our own business.'

'That doesn't sound so bad,' Grace replied.

'Maybe not, but my parents worried that I was throwing away my future for love which might not last.'

'Maybe they were worried about you,' Grace said. 'I know my parents are always worried, they're probably worried sick right now even though I did leave them a message.' Grace bit her lip, sudden anxiety flooding her body. She did feel guilty for causing her parents any unnecessary anxiety, but then she did not have any control over what they were thinking or feeling and she had tried her best to explain that she was ok in her message. Grace pushed any thoughts of her parents to one side.

'Yes, perhaps they were,' Josie said, her voice thoughtful.

'So you've got your own business,' Grace said, pointing around her to the house they were sitting in. 'But what happened with you and Owen? Did you break up?'

Josie stopped fiddling with her necklace abruptly, her face no longer thoughtful. Grace thought she could see her face closing off, like a shutter coming down over her features. She had unwittingly put her foot in it.

'I'm sorry—' but Josie interrupted her.

'There's nothing to be sorry for,' she said, her voice all business. 'Now then, if you have finished with your cake, I think I'll carry on with the housework,' she said, collected the plates and walked out of the room.

Grace sat back in her chair, puzzled. He must have broken her heart pretty badly, she thought and her thoughts strayed to Paul and she wondered whether she was currently breaking his heart by walking out of their love story and the life they shared.

*

Grace gratefully wrapped her cold fingers around the coffee mug, enjoying the warmth that immediately seeped into her frozen fingers. It was a cold, rainy day with a biting wind that felt like needles on the skin. Grace took a sip and smiled.

'Thanks, Holly, I needed this.'

'No problem,' Holly said and smiled, her tray on one hip, a dishcloth in her hand. The café seemed quiet today, which Grace put down to the rain. Who would want to go out in this? Grace herself had meant to only quickly nip out for some bits and pieces from town but the cold and rain had driven her towards Holly's café and much needed caffeine. Even though her recent decisions were meant to make her feel better, sleep still eluded Grace on most nights. She found herself lying in the dark, worrying, fretting over things, anxiety settling in her gut like a ton of bricks.

'Will you sit for a moment?' Grace gestured to the free chair on her table. 'If you have time that is?'

Holly sat down, settling the empty tray in front of her.

'I have a few minutes. As you can see there's not much going on today.'

'How are things?' Grace asked.

'Good thanks. The café is doing a bit better this month, so I'll be able to pay the bills, phew.' Holly mimicked wiping sweat from her forehead. Grace laughed.

'Surely the café is doing good on the whole? I mean who doesn't love this place? It's a staple of the community.'

'You'd think so but overheads are a killer and prices keep increasing, and I don't see most of my customers paying £6.50 for a coffee, do you?'

'No, I suppose not. There must be other ways to increase your takings? Have you thought of hosting events or something like that?'

Holly nodded. 'Yes, I did try that a few months back but the turnout wasn't great. But maybe I need to look into that again, use more social media to get the word out.' She furrowed her brow for a moment, thinking. 'Anyway, how are things with you? How's Josie?'

'I'm doing ok, thanks. I'm still not sleeping great but I suppose that's not surprising.'

'Have you thought about what you are going to do?'

Grace shook her head. 'It's funny really, I always had a plan, or rather there was always a plan. And now I have no plan and I thought it would feel liberating, exciting even.'

'Doesn't it?'

'Most of the time I just feel anxious and worried.'

'Do you think you would feel less anxious if you simply went back? I'm sure your boyfriend would be happy to see you. And your boss might give you your job back if they haven't replaced you. Stranger things have happened.'

Grace thought for a moment. 'I suppose that's true. But even though I feel anxious, I don't feel anxious enough to hightail it back home. I feel like maybe I just need to let things rest for the moment.'

'Sounds like a plan to me. And listen, you know I'm here if you need anything.'

'Thanks, Holly.'

'So how's Josie doing?'

'I think she is doing ok. We kind of got our little routine now that I am staying indefinitely and she doesn't seem to have many other guests at any one time. She talks about Owen a lot, I mean, initially she was very vague and closed off about it but every so often she mentions him and I got the feeling that she wants to talk about him, so every time I encourage her by asking something about him. Then again, maybe she is just trying to cheer me up—' Grace stopped mid-flow, suddenly becoming aware of Holly's expression.

'What's wrong? What did I say?'

'Nothing, you didn't say anything wrong. It's just Owen—'

'What about Owen? He sounds great, I wonder what happened between them. I know this might sound strange but Josie doesn't seem to be over him. Do you know him?'

'Grace,' Holly said, her voice slightly strained. 'I'm not sure I should be the one to tell you this—' Holly trailed off.

'Tell me what?'

After a moment Holly seemed to gather herself, taking a deep breath.

'Grace,' she said, 'Owen is dead.'

Chapter 4

Owen

I don't remember much of the crash itself. One minute I was driving along, perhaps slightly too fast, the visibility not great as rain pelted down on the windscreen, bouncing off the glass in a never ending pattern, the windscreen wipers working relentlessly in a forward and backward motion, sweeping the water away but not quite managing to catch up. It was dark, I was on my way home, anxious to get there.

The engagement ring burned a hole in my pocket. It had been a spontaneous purchase. Does anyone make this sort of decision spontaneously? I suppose so. You hear of people getting married after four weeks of knowing each other, whirlwind romances and the like. But this was different.

From the moment I met Josie, I knew I would want to marry her one day. But I hadn't planned when that day would be. In fact, marriage had never been that much on my mind. My parents had a happy marriage and I suppose I always thought that one day I would have that too. But actually making the decision to propose came as a surprise. I saw this ring, silver with a turquoise stone, and I suddenly thought, *This is the ring I'm going to propose to Josie with.* Out of the blue, just like that.

I'm a firm believer that things happen for a reason so I went inside and bought the ring. And then I just wanted to get home and present her with it. I wanted to see the look on her face when I said the words. I hoped she'd say yes. In fact I didn't know what I would do if she said no. I was fairly certain the answer would be yes. Josie is not one to shy away from an adventure.

Perhaps I was distracted, thinking about which words to use to convey my love for her. The joy of getting engaged and celebrating this step in our lives.

I didn't see the oncoming car, the driver struggling to control the car on the slippery, wet surface, until I was blinded by bright headlights. I don't remember much after that.

The next thing I know, I'm hovering over the grassy verge, feeling light and weightless. Above me there were clouds in the dark night sky but every now and again when they broke apart, I could see a twinkling light of a star. The rain was still falling but I couldn't feel it on my skin. I couldn't feel anything, which was odd. I looked down and I saw myself. My body tangled and twisted in the grass, my eyes closed. Panic gripped me. I didn't understand. What was I doing here when I was down there? Had I been literally split in two? How would I get back? As the panic took hold of me I had one thought and one thought only: Josie. Then everything went black.

A few metres away, a black velvety box lay open, the ring it held lying in the grass, lost. The rain continued to fall, oblivious to the lives that had been changed forever.

*

Since then not much has happened. I figured out pretty quickly that I had not survived the car crash. That is my body, because my mind or soul or whatever this is still remains. I believe the universal term for my condition is being a ghost.

I am a ghost.

If this wasn't actually the reality, I'd burst into laughter. Unfortunately nobody has left me a manual on how to be a ghost or what it involves or whether there is a way out of ghostness. Am I to be a ghost for eternity now?

I keep looking out for bright lights but there are none forthcoming. Initially I tried very hard to remember everything I ever knew about ghosts. Aren't they meant to have unfinished business? Well yeah I have unfinished business, I was in the middle of living my life! How am I supposed to resolve that?

After I blacked out, I came to in the living room. Of our house. On Mull. The move there had been arranged and was to take place in two weeks' time. Another reason why proposing seemed such a great idea. I had inherited the house when my parents died within two weeks of each other. It was a blow that I struggled to deal with, to lose both of them, too early in my and their life. My brother Sean worked and lived in Asia and the will stipulated that he was to receive his share of the house in money. Luckily my parents were good at saving money and we didn't have to deal with the stress of lengthy financial and legal complications.

I didn't know initially what to do with the house. I could never bear to sell it but to live there? In my childhood home?

Without my parents? It seemed unthinkably painful. It was Josie who opened my eyes. She had always had this idea of opening up a B&B, not just for anyone but for artists, writers and musicians, to create a haven where people could come together. Perhaps her own lonely childhood had something to do with the longing for a home and to share that home with others. She told me that we could make it my parents' legacy, we could honour their memory and suddenly the idea made sense.

Mull is a wild place and I longed for the open space and the ocean to heal the grief that threatened to overwhelm and swallow me whole and so I agreed and we put plans in place.

We would be starting a new chapter on Mull and what better way to begin our adventure with getting engaged? My thoughts immediately turned to Josie. Had she been told yet? How was she coping? For all her bravado, Josie could be quite fragile. She wouldn't allow anyone to see that except me. For some reason Josie allowed herself to be vulnerable with me and that was the greatest gift someone had ever given me.

And now I had left her. Not by choice but still, I was no longer alive. Sadness stole over me, quickly and intensely. I nearly passed out again.

Perhaps I could find a way to talk to her. In movies ghosts do this all the time so maybe there is some truth in that? Maybe I could start with tipping a vase off a book shelf or something to alert her to my presence. I looked around the living room. I spotted a glass coaster on the mantelpiece that my mother used to put tea lights on in the winter and for a moment I was transported back to the cosy winter evenings of my childhood, tea lights twinkling on the mantelpiece, a crackling fire in the log burner, Christmas around the corner. I took a deep breath and shook my head and the memory dissolved into tiny fragments.

I turned my attention to the glass coaster and tried swiping it off the mantel but nothing happened. Great. I couldn't even do that. I turned away in frustration. This was hopeless, absolutely hopeless. I didn't want this. I didn't choose this. Why am I stuck here? What a shitty situation to be in! Anger swept over me, hotly and quickly. Behind me I heard something shatter into a million pieces on the floorboards. I turned around and looked at the glass coaster, broken, its pieces glinting in the weak sunlight that was streaming through the windows.

I smiled. Perhaps all was not lost yet. I would wait for Josie and as soon as she got here, I would make my presence felt. There was hope.

As it turns out I waited for a very long time. For all the reasons I thought I knew Josie inside out, I had not anticipated one thing.

She never came.

Josephine (Josie) – Now

The rugged landscape opened up before them, the wind lifting her hair with fierce force through the open window, the waves crashing over the jagged rocks in their race towards the shore. Josie felt the impact of what her eyes saw as if someone had punched her in the stomach. For a moment she just stared straight ahead, breathless.

'Josie, why didn't you tell me that Owen is dead?' Grace had asked her, her eyes wide with concern. Josephine had felt the walls caving in as a wave of grief hit her so fiercely, she feared she would lose her balance. Even after all this time, it felt like someone twisting a knife in her gut. She had grabbed the back of a chair to steady herself. 'Because,' she began, her voice trembling, 'Owen's death was devastating.'

'You must have loved him very much,' Grace had replied, watching her. And suddenly Josephine had felt a great need to explain, to explain to this young woman who had walked into her life what Owen had meant to her.

'Yes, I loved him very much,' she had said, 'but it's more than that. Owen and I understood each other, effortlessly, sometimes without words. His death was… it changed me. I was suddenly a different person without him. It broke me.' Her voice had caught then, as the truth of her words, spoken out loud, reverberated around the room. Grace had rushed across the room and held her in her arms as Josephine allowed herself to weep. A door that she had kept closed for a long, long time was suddenly forced open and whilst a distant part of her was embarrassed about making a spectacle of herself, the larger part welcomed the tidal wave of emotion. It was freeing somehow. It felt like a release.

Grace had made them tea and Josephine had wiped her face after her tears subsided, Biscuit faithfully sitting on her feet, regarding her with sad and worried eyes.

'It's ok, old boy,' she had reassured him. 'Just an old woman weeping about the past.'

'Was there never anyone else?' Grace had asked. Josephine had shaken her head.

'Don't get me wrong, I'm human and there were times when I wanted company but I never allowed myself to be in a relationship. I just couldn't.' She had spoken about Owen then. About the plans they had made, about his smile and the way he could make her laugh. How at times he had infuriated her like no one else could. How they had been each other's everything. When Josie's parents had died, first her mother, then her father, Owen had been there alongside her when she tried to come to terms with the loss. Josie's relationship with her parents had been complicated, distant, she felt they never really understood her as a person. But to be left without them felt strange, scary. Suddenly she had no one in the world, she was an orphan and the possibility of reconciliation, of making amends, of building bridges, was lost to her forever. She had been angry and she remembered feeling betrayed by them as if they had chosen to leave her behind. Alone.

So she had clung to Owen, like someone lost at sea clings to a lifeboat. Their relationship had become stronger, deeper. They had loved each other fiercely, leaving little room for anyone else.

'We were going to live on Mull,' Josie had ventured, 'but then the accident happened...' her voice trailed off.

'So you've never been back there?'

'Never,' Josie had shaken her head. 'I couldn't. I felt like the island was such a big part of Owen, so entwined with his essence that to go there without him, seemed impossible. So we had a funeral here for him. Sean, his brother came over for two nights. I think some people travelled down from Scotland but I can't really remember.' The truth was that Josie had been numb with grief. She had sleepwalked through those first few weeks, had no real recollection of organising a funeral or who had attended. One minute her life was ahead of her full of sparkling opportunities, filled with love and laughter, the next Owen was dead, cremated and she had felt utterly and completely alone.

*

'We're here. Where to next?' Grace's voice interrupted her déjà vu. Josie glanced at the young woman behind the wheel of her Mini. Grace had insisted on driving all the way here even though Josie had assured her that she was still capable of driving long distances without any problems. Then again she hadn't expected to feel like this, seeing the unmistakable landscape, barely five minutes off the ferry.

'The house is that way,' Josie said with a lump in her throat. It had been a surprise to her when the house had come into her possession. She hadn't known that Owen had made a will; perhaps he had mentioned it and she had forgotten, too wrapped up in the present and in their love to consider a world without Owen in it. She couldn't put the pain she felt into words. Not only had she been robbed of Owen but also of their future on the island. Suddenly the house had seemed like a symbol of what she no longer had.

How long was it since she had been back? Years. An eternity. Too long.

Josie glanced down at the urn she held tightly in her lap. Grace followed her gaze. She put a hand on her arm, her gaze back on the winding road.

'Don't worry,' she said softly. 'I'm sure he'll be glad to be home.'

Josie raised her eyes, a small smile on her lips.

'Yes,' she said, her voice steady, 'I think you might be right.'

*

It hadn't been a conscious decision to hold on to his ashes. In the beginning she hadn't even known what Owen would have wanted, although deep down she probably could guess and the chances of that guess being right were pretty high. But Josie hadn't felt able to make that decision. In her grief-stricken mind, holding on the ashes also meant holding on to Owen. She didn't know at the time that it would take her almost a lifetime to bring him home. To bring them both home.

The fierce, determined girl she had been died with Owen. She was replaced by a broken woman who at some point decided to box up her grief and to shove it to the deepest corner of her mind and heart, not realising that the grief she couldn't face was eating away at her soul and had been doing so for a long time.

Now as the house, Owen's childhood home, came into view, that box cracked wide open and a complex tangle of emotions spilled out, leaving Josie instantly tearful and overwhelmed.

The house sat on a cliff top set away from the road, overlooking the sea. A grassy trail, which could only barely be described as a road, led to a gravelled forecourt. As Grace negotiated the path, Josie held her breath as the white washed house came into view. The roof looked intact from what she could make out but the house looked neglected. Neglected but not broken. Josie bit her lip, trying to stop the tears from falling.

The house stood solid as if waiting patiently for her return. Somehow Josie found the thought immensely comforting.

The front garden was overgrown and Josie assumed that the back garden was in much the same state. It desperately needed a green fingered touch. It needs Owen, Josie thought as pain seared through her. She closed her eyes for a moment, riding out the wave of pain, raw and gut wrenching, as memories washed over her. She didn't know if she could do this. She wanted to run far away, escape this horrible feeling that was all consuming.

Josie took a deep breath and steeled herself. It was time, she thought. There had been a time for running away. But she couldn't run forever. It was time for her to put on her big girl pants. She had read that expression somewhere recently. She remembered smiling and thinking, I like that.

It was time to face her demons. She owed that much to Owen. And she owed it to herself.

Grace ground to a halt and peered through the windshield.

'Wow Josie, it looks lovely,' she said, awed.

'It is,' Josie replied quietly. Grace waited for Josie to expand but when she didn't, she put on her most cheerful voice.

'Shall we go inside? I'd love a cup of tea.' Biscuit barked in agreement, panting noisily. They had to stop frequently on the journey for him to have a little walk and to relieve himself. Josie thought that Biscuit had dealt remarkably well with the long drive.

Grace knew this was a difficult trip for Josie. They stepped out of the car, Biscuit sniffing the air before running around the garden, exploring. Josie fumbled in her bag for the key and handed it to Grace. A turquoise stone dangled from the key ring.

'That's nice,' Grace remarked, stroking the smooth, cool stone. Josie merely nodded. She didn't have the energy to make small talk. Feelings and memories were rushing at her nineteen to the dozen. She gripped the urn tighter.

They went inside. The air smelled musty and several layers of dust coated everything. Grace peered into several rooms, trying to locate the kitchen. Josie headed straight for the living room, a bright space thanks to the two big windows overlooking the sea. Josie looked out at the ocean. The wind had calmed down and the water sparkled blue and turquoise beneath her. It was beautiful, like it always had been.

Silent tears flowed down her cheeks, unchecked.

'Welcome home, Owen,' she whispered. 'I'm sorry it took me this long.'

Owen

I always felt most at peace on the island. I don't know why. Yes it was where I grew up but back then I couldn't wait to get away, to explore the world and visit far flung places. I was seeking adventure and the island of Mull didn't seem big enough.

Now, so many years later, I have been to many places around the world, some stunning, others not so much, and I have come to realise that none of them feel like home. Maybe the ignorance of youth is such that we seek to go further afield, not knowing or appreciating what we have. And once we have seen what is out there, we are inexplicably drawn back to the places that mean something to us. The places that we were so quick to disregard, thinking the grass is greener on the other side. Perhaps this is how we learn, about ourselves, about life.

I have realised that there is no other place in the world like Mull. The landscape is so varied in its colours, the shades of blue of the ocean wrapping itself around the island, and even when the weather is shockingly bad this place still has its own kind of magic.

I think Josie instinctively understood this because shortly after we came here, we talked about nothing else but living on the island. We were going to buy a house, but then my parents died and I inherited my childhood home. We stayed in the house for my parent's funeral. It was well loved but in need of some repairs. Seeing the potential stirred a determination in me to bring the house back to life and for us to put our own stamp on it. Josie loved the house and I love her so the reasons I had for simply selling up dissolved into thin air.

Since I met Josie, all I wanted to do was to make her happy. I wanted to give her everything. And where better to do that than in the place that brings you peace and has its own kind of rules, away from the pressures of society which seems fast paced and relentless? Sometimes it even feels like the rest of the world can't touch you here, like you are safe, far away from everything.

I wanted that for us. I wanted us to be free to love and to live, to really live.

Josephine (Josie) – Now

The Black Cow Pub was the hub of the village where everyone gathered for special occasions and on most nights to have a chat and a glass of something, catching up on the local gossip. The food was pretty good too.

After Grace had carried their luggage into the house and did a quick sweep through the kitchen cupboards, which were unsurprisingly bare, Josie had decided they should get something to eat before stocking up at the local supermarket. Word would get out soon (it always did) that she was back and she would rather face the locals now, on her terms, than be caught out unawares. Why this mattered she wasn't quite sure.

They had left Biscuit at home with a bowl full of food that they had brought with them and he had been content, snoozing in front of the unlit fireplace, already at home in his new surroundings.

Josie took a deep breath before she pushed open the old wooden door, Grace following closely behind her. The place hadn't changed, not even a little bit. Everything looked exactly the same, even the door still creaked in a familiar way. There were wooden tables, benches and chairs alongside both walls leading to a cosy fireplace. The bar was to the left of the door, simple but well stocked, and the windows overlooked the harbour. Time stood still and Josie half expected to see Owen rounding the corner at any moment. She grimaced, closing her eyes briefly as the ever present pain coursed through her.

The pub wasn't busy and as they stood there, a sudden silence ensued as eyes swivelled in their directions, roaming over them like a hungry lion would with its prey. Josie lifted her chin and straightened her shoulders in response; there was still a rebel lurking in her somewhere.

'Josephine Taylor as I live and breathe,' a deep voice said into the silence. A tall, heavily built man stepped out from behind the bar wiping his hands on a dish towel. He was around Josie's age with dark curly hair and a beard, brown eyes widened in astonishment before crinkling up with warmth as he smiled down at her.

'Hi Johnny,' Josie replied, answering his smile with one of her own. She allowed him to hug her and was relieved to see that the other people in the pub seemed to lose interest and returned to their own conversations.

'I never thought I'd see you again,' he said, 'it's been a long time.'

'It has,' Josie answered as memories of nights spent in the pub with Owen and Johnny, laughing and drinking, assaulted her from all sides. The three of them had been good friends, spending a lot of time together. Being back here was a million times harder than she had expected.

Johnny, perhaps sensing her struggle, directed his gaze at Grace.

'And who is this?'

'This is Grace,' Josie introduced her. 'She's a very good friend.'

'Hi, it's nice to meet you,' Grace said politely, shaking Johnny's hand.

'Likewise,' he replied, but his gaze had already returned to Josie.

'You look good.' Josie merely nodded her acknowledgment of the compliment. 'Are you guys hungry?'

'Starving,' Grace blurted out and Johnny laughed. He handed her two menus.

'Pick any table you like and I'll take your order in a moment.'

Josie was about to follow Grace when Johnny grabbed her hand.

'I was sorry to hear about Owen,' he said quietly. Josie nodded, not trusting herself to speak. 'It broke my heart. He was one of the best.' Johnny's eyes had grown misty.

'I know,' Josie replied softly. 'I brought him home, Johnny. I'm sorry it took me so long.' Tears trickled down Josie's cheeks and she rubbed at them with her hands, feeling irritated with herself. Crying in public, really?!

He nodded. 'What changed?' he asked.

Josie looked at Grace who was now seated at one of the tables, studying the menu. Johnny followed her gaze.

'Grace,' she said, 'and I don't know, it felt like it was time.'

Johnny put an arm around her and gave her a squeeze. Even though she had not seen him for years, Josie felt the comforting warmth of their friendship and smiled.

'Listen up everyone,' Johnny shouted and silence ensued once more. 'The next round is on the house in memory of my good friend Owen, who left us way too soon.'

'To Owen,' the people cheered and applauded. Despite herself Josie laughed. There were only a handful of people but she appreciated the gesture.

Still the same old Johnny, she thought.

Grace

Grace saw them looking at her shortly before Johnny made the announcement. She wondered what they were talking about, catching up probably.

Grace returned her attention back to the menu, trying to decide what to have. The pub was nice. It must be weird for Josephine to be back on old, familiar ground after a lifetime away. As far as she could gather Josie and Owen had spent a lot of time on the island with it being Owen's home turf.

Grace could already understand why, even though she'd only really been here five minutes. But the island was beautiful and there was a certain calmness here, a slower pace of life. The roads were quiet and nobody seemed in much of a hurry. It forced you to slow down too, to stay in the moment and the things that usually were heavy on her heart and mind seemed far away.

Or maybe she was just running away from her own problems. Grace sighed. Since meeting Josie, she had thrown herself into helping her. This trip had been her idea. As soon as Josie had told her about Owen and confessed that she still had his ashes, Grace had suggested they make the journey to Mull. She wanted to give Josephine a chance for closure and with that a chance to move forwards rather than being stuck in the debris of her broken dreams. Josie had been incredibly reluctant at first but after a few days of carefully considering the idea, she had agreed.

And yet the irony did not escape Grace. She had walked out of her life and was so far avoiding thinking about what she would do next. Would she go back?

Would she do something that was completely different?

She had no idea. She was stuck in no man's land.

And yet wasn't that the point? To take the time to get to grips with her own processes, her own way of feeling, thinking and seeing the world?

She was avoiding that too. Her voicemail had filled up with messages she didn't want to listen to. Luckily on this island, phone signal was like the holy grail, elusive and hard to find. Another advantage of making the trip.

Josie was a very perceptive lady and had already made several comments on Grace's apparent avoidance to deal with things. Grace knew that there would come a point where she could no longer keep running and she needed to face the reality of what she had done. You couldn't just walk away from everything and expect things to run smoothly.

At the same time she felt free, able to decide things for herself even if they were little things. Like the clothes she was wearing. Or the music she listened to. Or right now, what she was going to eat.

She smiled. Yes, there would come a point when she had to face the tough questions.

But right now wasn't it.

Right now she would enjoy eating a burger with extra cheese and a whole load of fries.

Chapter 5

Grace

Grace didn't know when she had first started to feel like something was wrong. It hadn't been like a gut wrenching, life changing lightbulb moment. It had been more like an inkling, a sense that something wasn't quite right. But that something was vague and distant.

It was persistent though.

Grace had carried on as normal, working in a job that felt ok but didn't set her soul on fire, going home to Paul, who was grounded and safe and treated her nicely, and going to dinner once a week with her parents, who encouraged others to make decisions for Grace amid the constant refrain of 'Oh Grace, you're so indecisive.' Indecisive, yes.

Incapable of making a decision?

Was that even the same thing? Did she choose not to choose?

She had felt tired, exhausted in fact. Her life had been like a hamster wheel, round and round in an endless loop of people-pleasing and deference because that was who she was and that was what she had always done. It was the nature of things.

Or was it?

Grace couldn't pinpoint the moment when she had started to question things. Was it when Connor, an arrogant, noisy colleague talked over her again at the weekly team meeting? Was that one too many times?

Or was it when Paul had picked the destination for their annual holiday without discussing it with her because, oh yes, she was indecisive and at the end of the day, didn't he know best?

Or was it when her mother oh so subtly told her during their last telephone conversation that Grace needed to think about having children because after all she wasn't getting any younger and wouldn't Paul feel more encouraged to pop the question if she was carrying his child?

And Grace had felt that little vague, distant but persistent inkling turn into something else entirely.

Anxiety.

Breathtaking, 'I can't do this anymore' anxiety that left no room for doubt or insecurity.

'Shut up, Connor, for once in your miserable life! No Mother, I do not want to have children right now, and no Paul I do not want to go to fucking Bali for two weeks! No! No! No!' her voice screamed loud and clear in her head.

So clear in fact that Grace had been startled. That's when she had known something had to change.

And in a moment of clarity, Grace had listened to her inner voice.

For the first time in her life.

'Think I can't make a decision?' it said. 'Watch me.'

*

And look at me now, she thought. Once she made the decision, the rest had come easily, almost too easily. She had handed in her notice, her boss suitably shocked, even more so when she told him she would not be working her notice period. She had driven home, giddy with relief and excitement.

At home she had packed a bag before sitting down and writing a letter to Paul. She had picked up said bag and turned at the front door to take a last look at the house that had been her home for the last three years.

She had felt nothing.

It only confirmed her decision. Images of the night before flickered in her mind, searing, painful. She had pushed them away, squeezing her eyes shut for a moment.

Then, she had pulled the door closed and locked it. She had walked towards her car before suddenly hesitating. The small Vauxhall Corsa in demure silver was practical, sensible and reliable. All the things she supposedly was. Something in Grace rebelled.

She shook her head, straightened her shoulders and without a backwards glance had walked away from the house, the car, her life as she knew it.

*

Now she was walking on a stony pathway towards what Josie had promised her was a stunning beach, on an island she had never heard of, with Josie, who was practically a stranger, walking beside her. Biscuit was running up ahead, tongue lolling, enjoying himself.

It was crazy!

And yet she felt completely calm.

She felt free.

Suddenly her life was her own. Every decision, every action she took was her own. It was breathtaking and terrifying in equal measures. And whilst her anxiety still lingered, it was no longer crushing and all consuming.

It was their third day on the island.

Josie had felt exhausted on the evening of their arrival and they had spent the last two days cleaning the house and stocking up on everyday essentials. Josephine had been back to the Black Cow Pub to spend some time with Johnny and to catch up on years of missed friendship.

This morning they had taken the ferry across to Iona. Josie had explained that Iona was very special and pilgrims had long since made their way to its shores. It was a holy and spiritual place. In AD 563, the monk Columba had arrived on the island to spread the gospel. He built a church and established a community of monks. Josie had pointed out the restored abbey that stood proudly in the sunshine.

It was a beautiful building and no doubt the reason for the coachload of tourists that would descend upon the small island come the afternoon. Josie had insisted that they make the journey early in the morning to avoid the crowds.

Grace wrapped her scarf tighter around her neck. Even though the sun was shining and the sky was blue, the wind still held a bitter chill to it. As her gaze wandered across the landscape, she couldn't help but think that she understood why people thought this was a spiritual place. There was a calmness here, a peacefulness that enveloped her like a much needed hug.

They walked past green fields, the odd Scottish Highland cow blinking at them. Grace had been initially concerned that Josie might struggle, but since they had arrived in Scotland Josie seemed more energetic somehow, like she was drawing strength from being somewhere so strongly connected to Owen.

Slowly the path gave way to a grassy lane before changing again into dunes. They followed the path before walking through a wooden gate. Grass became golden, dusty sand underneath their walking boots.

'Wow look at this sand,' she exclaimed.

Josie chuckled.

'Wait until you see the beach,' her voice was filled with a youthful excitement.

They slowly descended the dune before stepping onto a long, sandy stretch of beach, punctuated by the black and purple rocks Grace already associated with the Ross of Mull. The water glinted in blue and turquoise shades and the waves gently lapped at the shore, despite the wind. Grace took a moment to take it all in.

'It's stunning,' she breathed.

Josie smiled. 'Owen and I came here a lot. Come, let's walk a little bit further, I know a place that's quite sheltered from the wind.'

They fell into step beside each other in companionable silence, each lost in their own thoughts. Grace thought that Josephine seemed to feel closer to Owen here than at home. Presumably because at home she had tried to keep the lid firmly on the box that held her grief and her memories. Theirs must have been a strong, enduring kind of love.

Passionate, full of adventure.

Unwittingly images of Paul danced before her inner eye. Paul who was excessively tidy, who planned everything within an inch of its life and who was a natural leader. Grace had felt safe with him. He had radiated security and it had been a nice feeling to be taken care of, to feel protected, for things to follow a predictable pattern. Sex on Tuesday and Fridays and maybe Saturday if they were pushing the boat out. Sundays they would hit the gym and go out for a late breakfast and at some point Thursdays had become steak night.

Predictable. Safe.

Until it had become stifling.

Grace wrinkled her nose. She didn't even know if she liked steak.

But Paul was not the type of man who adapted easily to change and the few times she had tried to give voice to her emerging feelings, he had become frustrated and irritable. Paul didn't understand why she could possibly be unhappy with the life they were leading. At the time she had felt guilty, ashamed even. She had a lot of things other people would love to have. But as she tried to go back to feeling content, the feelings of being stifled, contained, trapped intensified and left her breathless with panic. It was as if the tapestry of her life had been ripped apart and she could no longer fit the pieces together as they had been. Something new, unknown was emerging.

She wondered what Paul was doing now? The phone signal on Mull was terrible and perhaps that in it itself was a blessing in disguise. Paul would want her to come back and she was sure he didn't understand what she was doing, he probably thought she was having some sort of breakdown. Maybe she was, although it didn't feel like she was losing her mind. Not anymore. It was the opposite in fact. She felt like she was finally seeing sense, finding herself, getting to know who she truly was as a person away from what everyone else wanted her to be. Was he missing her? Was she missing him?

She shook her head to disperse the thoughts, the images. She didn't want to think about this right now. Grace took a breath and tried to ground herself in the here and now. On her walking boots crunching the golden sand beneath her feet. On the sound of the waves. On the wind that gently lifted her hair. On Josie who was walking beside her, hands in her pocket, a faraway look on her face, no doubt lost in her own memories.

She focused her eyes on Biscuit, who was racing down the beach, sand flying from his paws, barking at the waves as they came rushing to meet him. She smiled. Josie followed her gaze.

'That dog is a joy to watch,' she said.

Grace agreed.

A short while later Josephine led them onto a part of the rocks that was sheltered from the wind. The stone was smooth and surprisingly comfortable to sit on. Josie reached into her pocket and called to Biscuit, who came running towards them. She fed him a couple of dog biscuits, which he gratefully accepted, lowering himself to the ground beside them. Josie passed Grace a chocolate bar before unwrapping her own.

'For sustenance,' she said.

They looked out to sea and Grace enjoyed the flavour of chocolate and caramel. Back home, she ate a very healthy diet.

'Tell me about you and Owen,' she said after a moment.

'Did you know that Scotland had beaches like this?' Josie asked.

Grace shook her head.

Josie smiled a wistful smile. 'That's Scotland for you. Always has a surprise up its sleeve.'

She remained silent for a moment.

'And so did Owen.'

Josephine (Josie) – Then

Tires screeching, she flew down the road, her foot firmly pressed onto the accelerator. The car roared in response, a satisfying rumbling sound, like a lion's roar, ready for battle, ready for anything.

Oh she was so mad! How dare he do this to her? After everything they'd been through. After all the heartache, he wanted there to be more. Not on her watch though, she wasn't having any of it!

Josie changed gears, her fingers gripping the steering wheel of her Ford Cortina as she raced down roads and finally the stretch of motorway that would lead her to Owen's house. Her heart was racing in her chest as the adrenaline fuelled through her. He drove her insane sometimes but this time he had truly outdone himself.

Owen was tall, handsome in a not too obvious way and

fiercely intelligent and she had fallen head over heels in love with him the first time their paths crossed and his grey green eyes had met her blue ones. His smile was damn sexy but his laugh, a low chuckle, knocked her feet right out underneath her.

They had a lot of chemistry, they knew it and everyone around them knew it. Owen and Josie were destined to be together and as a couple they were an unstoppable force, full of energy, passion, heading for great things. But that passion also meant that they clashed at times and their arguments tended to be fierce, neither of them holding back, both of them believing to be in the right, wanting to confront the other with the truth. Not that they argued a lot, but when they did it wasn't pretty and it sure as hell wasn't easy.

Josie screeched to a halt before his house, slammed her car door with more force than strictly necessary and marched into Owen's house without knocking.

'Owen!' she bellowed, 'where the hell are you and what the hell are you playing at?'

Owen appeared in the kitchen doorway, in jeans and a black t-shirt, looking insanely and annoyingly handsome. This whole debacle clearly hadn't affected his beauty sleep. *Well good for bloody you,* Josie seethed inwardly. 'Josephine,' Owen's voice was calm but cold, 'come on in why don't you?'

Josie narrowed her eyes. He only called her Josephine when he was annoyed at her.

'Do you want to explain to me what the hell you are doing, interfering in my business?' she cut to the chase. Owen sighed but didn't break eye contact.

'You call it interfering, I call it looking out for you!'

'Looking out for me?' Josie replied, her voice two octaves higher than normal. 'I don't need you or any man for that matter looking out for me! I know perfectly well what I'm doing!'

'Whatever! I know you don't want to face facts but the fact is that your business idea is vague. You have no clue how to run a business, let alone set one up, and that deal you were about to make? With that piteous clown who can't sell a cow to a milkman? Let's just say I've saved you from making the biggest mistake of your life. You can thank me later.'

Josie stared back at him, her mouth open in disbelief at his audacity.

'What the actual fuck, Owen?'

Their eyes locked for a long moment, before Owen walked back into the kitchen and reappeared a few moments later with a file of paperwork.

'Here,' he said, handing the file to Josie. 'Read this. It's all in there, the guy is a schmuck. You would have lost everything with no way of making it right.'

Owen's face softened, sparking more fury in Josie. She didn't want his pity, she didn't need it.

'You think you know everything, don't you?' she spat, venom in her voice, but she took the file. Although she felt like she wanted to murder him right now, she trusted Owen without a shadow of a doubt, always had done and always would. That didn't mean she thought he knew what was best for her, nobody got to make that choice for her.

Not anymore.

'Stop being childish, Josie,' he muttered, 'I'm trying to help you here.'

'I don't need your help,' she retaliated, even though she knew that wasn't entirely true. And so did he.

'You know what, Josie?' he said, angry now, his patience running out. 'You're nothing but a cowboy-boots-wearing wannabe who is pushing everyone away on some misguided vendetta to prove to everyone that you know what you're doing. But you don't. For God sake's open your eyes!'

Josie looked down at her worn leather cowboy boots. She loved those boots. Not only were they super comfy but they also made her feel confident.

'What? They're awesome boots and besides—' she hesitated.

'Besides what?' Owen asked.

'Besides, I'm not like anybody else,' Josie replied, suddenly deflated.

Owen cracked a smile and it was like the hallway in which they were standing arguing, was suddenly flooded with sunshine.

'No Josie, you got that one right, you're certainly nothing like anybody I've ever met.'

Josie looked at the file of papers in her hand, her anger rushing back at her like a tidal wave and like always, Josie wanted to have the last word.

'Do you know what, Owen?' she said. 'Screw you!' and without so much as a backward glance, she walked out, slamming the door shut behind her.

*

Josie kept glancing at the file of papers on her passenger seat. Her anger had slowly but surely ebbed away and had made space for reason to get a word in edgeways.

'You're too fiery,' she heard her mother's voice. 'It's going to get you into trouble and before you know it people will think you actually are trouble.'

Josie sighed. Didn't she just know it. Damn you, Owen, she swore and slammed the steering wheel with her hand before pulling her beloved Cortina off the road and hitting the brake pedal. She took a moment to calm her thoughts before grabbing the file and starting to read through the carefully compiled papers, absentmindedly brushing away a strand of her hair. Owen had said her business idea was vague but Josie had done her research and felt that a scented candle and soap business might just take off. Times were changing and people wanted thoughtful and ethically made gifts. Josie loved crafting and resented having to work in an office, slaving away for someone else's benefit nine to five. Owen, who had always had steady work, didn't understand why she couldn't do the candle-making as a side hustle to her current job. She could hardly tell him because she didn't want to. He would only call her childish again. Her cheeks flamed from the insult. He knew which buttons to press.

After what felt like a long time, Josie's anger made a reappearance, but this time it was directed at the ball of slime of a man called Patrick Peterson.

'It's a sure thing,' he had said. 'It's a fantastic idea and we will make this happen.' He'd assured her using phrases like minimum risk and client-centred repayment options. Josie had felt vindicated and excited, finally getting a loan to start up her very own business. No more nine-to-five for her, no Sir!

But the reality was that she would have lost everything if she was unable to keep up with the payments due to a tiny clause in the contract that stipulated the interest was to be doubled every few months. She would have been left with a mountain of debt that might as well be Everest for all the hope she would have had of paying it off.

What an absolute asshole, she thought, gritting her teeth. She stared out of the windscreen, miles of road ahead of her.

In her mind's eye she saw her future crumbling into a cloud of dust. Tears pricked her eyes unexpectedly but she blinked them away. She would get there. Somehow. She wouldn't give up. Not yet.

She started the car and did a U-turn, driving back the way she had come an hour or so ago. She had an apology to make and with renewed energy she pressed the accelerator.

Owen

The day I gave Josie those papers I had collated was another day on which we argued. Part of me had known she would react this way, defensive, quick to challenge, fiery. That was Josie all over. Even in her fury she was still stunningly beautiful. To me she always would be.

Lately, Josie had been trying to find her place in the world, to make her mark with a determination and drive that left me breathless at times. I hate to admit this but I also felt scared. Scared that somehow our relationship, what we shared, wasn't enough for her, that changing my life for the better didn't cut it. I guess I was scared that she would leave to pursue bigger and better things. Maybe that was also partly why I looked into things in the first place, though I like to believe that the main reason was to protect her. For all her determination Josie could be painfully naïve. A lot of the time she drove me nuts.

'Love's like that, mate,' my friend Johnny told me once when we were having a pint in our local when I was visiting my parents on Mull.

Josie had come up with this idea for a candle and soap-making business. Josie loved to be creative and I knew she hated the job she was working in. She felt stifled. But her business acumen wasn't great and she would have lost almost everything had I not intervened. But Josie was also a proud woman so she was never going to take my interference lightly. Once she had stormed out of my house, I had gone back to working on one of the kitchen cupboards. The kitchen needed a bit of an overhaul but as money was tight I had decided to repaint the kitchen cupboards, thinking it would give the whole room a bit of a lift.

It was perhaps an hour later when she walked back in, the file under her arm and a box in her hands.

'I'm sorry,' she said. 'I should really learn to listen, shouldn't I?'

'That's one way of putting it,' I replied, a small smile forming on my lips.

'I love you,' she said throwing her arms around me.

'And,' she said with a smile, 'I brought cake. Apology cake,' she said and laughed.

What can I say? Most of the time life with Josie was sweet.

Josephine (Josie) – Then

Betty's was a rickety looking building, not far from the main port where the ferries crossed over from the mainland. Owen had told her that it was tradition in his family for the first stop upon returning to the island to be at Betty's. He had a mischievous glint in his eye when he had told her this and Josie bit her lip now as she looked at the place. Through the window she could see a small room with tables and chairs and a counter at the back.

'Come on,' Owen said and took her hand, pulling her towards the entrance.

It was only her second time on the Isle of Mull and she wondered why they hadn't stopped here the first time Owen brought her home to meet his family. Perhaps they had both been nervous. Meeting your boyfriend's parents for the first time was nerve racking and Owen had mainly dated girls from the island whom he more or less grew up with. It had been the first time he was bringing home a girl from the mainland and Josie had tried hard to put any feelings of being an outsider out of her mind. She couldn't change who she was and she had realised with stunning clarity that she didn't want to. If only Mrs Winter had still been alive, Josie could have asked her for advice or some words of comfort and wisdom. But Mrs Winter had been dead a long time and so Josie was left to navigate her nerves on her own.

In the end, all of her worries had been unnecessary. Owen's parents were warm, friendly people. Clearly used to all sort of antics from raising two boys, they had welcomed her into their noisy, lived in, animals-everywhere home as if she had always belonged there. It was obvious how much Owen's parents loved him and his brother, and Josie had tried hard to swallow the unexpected lump that had formed in her throat. It was such a different experience to her own family, in which her parents loved her in their own peculiar and distant way. She did feel incredibly lonely sometimes. She swallowed and forced herself to focus on the present.

Owen pushed open the door and Josie looked at the things on offer. Homemade cakes and shortbread took pride of place in the glass counter alongside handmade chocolates.

'You're better not planning on sitting in, I'm practically closed,' a stern looking woman reprimanded them. She was short and stocky with a round face, her brown hair swept into a severe bun and a sparkling white apron tied around her not inconsiderable waist. Brown eyes stared at them before they narrowed slightly.

'Ah come on, Betty,' Owen said and smiled his most dazzling smile. 'You and I both know you've got at least another half an hour on the clock. Besides it's only your favourite customer ever and,' he nodded towards Josie, 'I'm trying to impress, come on, help a guy out.'

Josie watched the exchange, secretly worried that Owen had taken it too far. Betty looked like she was about to scream blue murder.

'You're a cheeky sod, Owen McGregor,' she said, grumbling. 'Make it quick then,' she said, to Josie's surprise.

Owen ordered two hot chocolates to go.

'Say hello to your mam,' Betty told him instead of saying goodbye. Owen raised his takeaway cup in reply.

'Thanks Betty,' he said. 'You're a star!'

Once outside and out of earshot, they both burst out laughing.

'Oh my God,' Josie said, 'I thought she was going to kill you. The look she gave you—'

Owen laughed. 'Nah, Betty's ok, she's one of a kind. Cheers!' he said and bumped his takeaway cup against hers.

They crossed the road and sat on a bench, overlooking the water. Josie took a sip of her hot chocolate and closed her eyes in appreciation. It tasted of deep dark chocolate with a hint of hazelnut.

'Amazing!' she said. Owen beamed at her.

'The thing about Betty is,' he said, 'she might be grumpy but her hot chocolate is truly divine.'

*

Josie blinked, looking down at the sponge in her hand. Her mind had wandered as she was cleaning the upstairs bathroom. The memory had come to her unbidden, rising out of the depths of her subconscious. It happened more and more since she had returned to the island as if a key had turned in a lock, opening a door that had been firmly shut for a long time. Too long perhaps.

She wondered where Betty was now. Josie remembered that Betty had had a soft spot for Owen, his cheekiness and daring. They had been to the café many times together, buying coffee and cake, having an impromptu picnic in the park across the road.

Josie rinsed out the sponge in the now clean sink and put

the bathroom cleaner spray bottle back into the cupboard underneath it. When she and Grace had first arrived on Mull, she had felt so overwhelmed and emotional that it never occurred to her to stop at Betty's. She wondered if the café was still there and what had happened to Betty. She dried her hands and walked out of the room. Only one way to find out.

'Biscuit,' she called and patted him on the head as he came trotting towards her, wagging his tail.

'Do you fancy going on an adventure down memory lane?'

Chapter 6

Grace

Grace looked at the small boat rocking precariously in the harbour with dubious eyes and a sinking feeling in her stomach. Right now she was starting to regret that she had agreed to take this day trip.

On her own.

'Oh but you must go and see Staffa Island,' Josie had urged her. 'It is the most amazing place and you might even get to see some puffins. Now, they are delightful creatures. I would go with you but I'm afraid my sea legs have deserted me in my old age.'

Grace doubted whether she herself had sea legs, only having been on a boat a handful of times in her life.

'All right then, all aboard,' the guy in charge instructed her and a handful of other people waiting in line to embark.

Josie had advised her to take the morning trip as it was likely the coaches would arrive for the afternoon journey and being squashed into a boat like Sardines appealed even less to Grace.

She followed the people in front of her but as she stepped onto the deck, a wave suddenly rocked the boat and she lost her footing.

'Whoa, don't fall,' a male voice said, strong arms reaching out for her and stopping her from falling. Grace looked up, her face flushing red from embarrassment, into a pair of green, friendly eyes.

'I'm so sorry,' she mumbled.

'Don't be,' the man replied, flashing a smile and after making sure she had regained her balance, letting go of her. She swallowed and sat down quickly, looking out at the water, trying to mask her embarrassment.

Today, the sea seemed choppy as a cool wind swept across the water. The sky was cloudy and Grace felt grateful for the extra layer she had decided to put on this morning. Out of the corner of her eye she watched the man who had come to her rescue, securing ropes and going through various safety checks. He was well built, with dark cropped hair and a face that wasn't traditionally handsome but that appealed to Grace. And those eyes. Grace felt herself blush again and quickly banished the thought.

The other member of staff was older and seemed to be in charge. When everyone was seated, the older man introduced himself as Bill, the captain, and referred to the younger one as Tom. Grace guessed him to be around her age. Bill talked them through the emergency protocol whilst expertly steering the boat out onto the open water. Spray sprinkled her face as the wind whipped around them, waves slapping the boat as it made its way towards Staffa Island. Grace gripped the rail, her knuckles white, but after a while she relaxed, feeling reassured by Bill's steady hand on the wheel, pushing the boat forwards towards their destination.

Grace saw seabirds swooping down into the waves only to

emerge moments later, searing into the sky, sometimes a fish clasped in their beaks. After the best part of an hour or so the island of Staffa came into view with its majestic columns rising out of the water, surrounding the open mouth of Fingal's Cave. The island was uninhabited and home to a variety of wildlife, mainly seabirds and puffins, Bill informed them.

Bill steered the boat into a small cove and explained that this was the only place where the boat could drop them off and pick them back up again. After securing the ropes, Tom helped everyone disembark the boat. Grace tried and failed to ignore the quickening of her heartbeat as Tom's hand firmly gripped hers as she stepped on land. Steep steps had been carved into the cliff and she followed the rest of the group as they climbed towards a small platform. Most of the group decided to head towards the cave first but Grace decided against visiting the echoing cavern and carried on climbing the steps.

Oh God, she thought, out of breath and sweating. No one had mentioned the amount of stairs she would have to climb. Her legs burned as she continued to climb towards the top. *I am so unfit,* she thought, hands on her knees, as she took a moment to catch her breath. Before her a grassy landscape stretched out in front of her. There were no trees, allowing her eyes to travel across the expanse. 'Wow,' Grace said out loud. The views were stunning. Surrounded by the sea, which looked much calmer from up here, Staffa Island contrasted the blue with the deep green of its grassland and black rocks. Grace set off towards the point Bill had advised them was the best place to see puffins.

Grace relished the solitude of walking alone, at her own pace, letting her thoughts drift and wander where they pleased. She was so lost in her thoughts that she didn't notice Tom catch up with her and nearly jumped out of her skin when he said a cheery hello.

'Jesus wept,' she exclaimed, clutching her chest. Tom laughed, a deep, throaty laugh and held up his hands in apology.

'I'm sorry,' he said, 'I didn't mean to scare you.'

'No harm done,' Grace replied and felt herself blushing again, much to her embarrassment.

'Are you looking for puffins?' Tom fell into step beside her.

'Yes. Bill said earlier that there is a particular point on the island where they like to congregate? Speaking of which, shouldn't you be with him?'

'I'm on my break. Bill's on the boat, having a cuppa. I'm Tom by the way,' he said holding out his hand.

'Grace,' she replied, shaking his hand.

'So Grace,' Tom said, 'I know Bill sends all the tourists up here but I know a secret spot if you want to get up close and personal.'

'I beg your pardon? What the hell? You're not seriously propositioning me right now, are you?' Grace felt anger bubble up inside her and rapidly reviewed her options in her mind. She could run and scream for help but then he hadn't actually done anything.

Yet.

Given her current state of fitness it might be difficult to outrun him but if she took him by surprise she might have a head start.

His rich deep laugh interrupted her escape plans.

'Gosh, that's not at all what I meant,' Tom said, his eyes creased up in laughter. 'I meant close and personal to the puffins.'

Seeing her face, Tom became serious. 'I mean it. I don't proposition our clients, otherwise I'd be out of a job. I can go back to the boat if that would make you feel more comfortable.'

Grace took in his body language and felt the colour rise in her face again. How many times was she going to embarrass herself in front of this guy? Of course he wasn't propositioning her, why would he?

'No that's ok,' she said and after a brief pause. 'I'd love to see the puffins.'

'Great,' Tom said, smiling. 'Follow me.'

'But no funny business,' Grace warned. 'I know self-defence.'

Tom laughed. 'No funny business. Cross my heart,' he said whilst actually making a crossing gesture over his heart.

They walked a little bit further up the path before Tom pointed to a small walkway leading halfway down the rocky cliff.

'Watch your step,' he instructed her and Grace carefully followed him down the grassy verge. Tom turned around and held out his hand to help her step onto a small ledge of rock sticking out from the cliff. She could hear the waves crashing onto the rocks beneath them. One wrong step and she would tumble into the vast ocean below. Tom put a finger to his lips and pointed. Grace's eyes followed where Tom was pointing to and there on a ledge sat two puffins.

Grace held her breath as she gazed at the beautiful birds, named the clowns of the sea due to their colourful beaks and big feet. They seemed curious as they watched them with black, intelligent eyes.

Grace's fingers itched to take out her phone to capture the moment but she worried that any movement might startle the birds into taking flight. Tom, as if reading her mind, slowly and without taking his eyes off the two puffins, slipped his phone out of his coat pocket and expertly took a photo. Her eyes met his and they shared a smile, revelling in this beautiful moment.

Grace didn't know how long they stood there watching the birds but when they heard voices overhead, Tom signalled that it was time to head back.

'Otherwise this spot will no longer be a secret,' he whispered to Grace.

'Wow, that was amazing,' Grace exclaimed once they were back on the grassy path at the top of the island.

'You're very welcome,' Tom replied. 'Hey if you give me your number I can send you that photo if you like.'

Grace hesitated.

'Don't worry, I'm not propositioning you,' he added with a smile, picking up on her hesitation.

Grace stuck her tongue out at him but she was already reaching for her cross body bag to extract her phone. They swapped numbers.

'Would you like to go for a drink with me sometime?' Tom asked after a short while.

Grace glanced at him. 'I thought you weren't pro-positioning me?' she asked.

'I'm not.' Tom smiled. 'I'm asking you out.'

A million reasons raced through Grace's mind to say no. Technically she was still in a relationship for one. Also she didn't know anything about Tom. Maybe he did this with all the tourists who took his fancy. It was not the sensible thing to do.

But then Grace wasn't here to be sensible. Hadn't she followed Josie to this island in the middle of nowhere on a whim? Josie, who was also practically a stranger?

Grace was here to find herself, to find her own path, to figure out her life. Sensible didn't cut it. Not anymore. It was time to do things differently.

'Ok. Yes, I'll go for a drink with you.'

Tom's delighted face made her smile.

Yes, she thought, *why the hell not?*

Josephine (Josie) – Now

Josie walked around the house. It was a cool morning but there was no rain and the wind had dropped. Pale sunlight filled the rooms, dipping everything into a watery golden light. Biscuit was snoozing in front of the unlit fireplace in the living room, his large body curled up on a shaggy, cosy rug. Josie envied him his ability to nod off effortlessly, giving himself completely to the joys of uninterrupted sleep. She herself was not so lucky and had barely slept since they arrived on Mull. Memories assaulted her at every corner and her aching bones made it difficult to find comfort in the wide bed she should have been sharing with Owen for all these years.

She sighed and wandered into the kitchen to make some coffee. Grace had left early with Tom to visit Duart Castle. The two of them seemed to be spending a lot of time together since they met three days ago and Josie knew without a shadow of a doubt that Tom had taken a liking to Grace. What guy wouldn't? She was pretty, intelligent and had an excellent sense of humour. Josie smiled. Sometimes it astonished her that she hadn't known Grace for long. It seemed to her like they had known each other for ages.

But Josie felt worried too. Grace was running from her life. She had left her job, her relationship, her family behind her. She was trying to find herself, to figure out who she was as a person and what she wanted from her life but that didn't mean that her boyfriend or her family had left her. Things were never that black and white. And Josie knew from experience that you couldn't run forever. The irony of her current circumstances wasn't lost on her.

Josie unearthed the coffee and spooned some into a glass cafétière before filling the kettle with water. It was strange. Since she was back on the island, she seemed to feel so much closer to Owen.

It was years ago now since he unexpectedly died in that terrible car accident and yet she had never been able to move forwards. Not really. She had existed, yes. But her life had ended as much as his did on that rainy, dark evening that still filled her with shivering dread whenever she allowed herself to think about it. Without him nothing had made sense. It still didn't.

And yet here, in this house, she felt him everywhere. She couldn't explain it. The boiling kettle startled her and she shook herself out of her reverie. You silly old woman, she reprimanded herself. Stop being so sentimental. She poured water into the cafétière and waited a few minutes before pushing the plunger down. The aroma of coffee filled the air, comforting and familiar. Josie poured herself a cup, adding milk and took the first, blissful sip, her eyes closed.

'You haven't changed a bit.'

Josie's eyes snapped open, her hands shaking. The voice had been crystal clear and yet there was no one else in the kitchen.

She would know his deep, baritone voice anywhere. Even after all these years. The hairs on the back of her neck stood up.

'Owen?' she whispered into the silence.

Grace

Grace looked at the landscape racing past the window. Green, purple and blue, so many shades of blue. There were fields, towering hills and always a glimpse of the sea or a loch around the next corner. The island of Mull had its own, unique charm, its rugged and beautiful landscape imprinting itself onto her heart. She felt far away here, enhancing her sense of escaping her problems.

Grace turned her gaze to the man next to her, sitting behind the wheel of a battered Land Rover in a faded forest green. His fingers lay relaxed around the wheel, his green eyes steady and focused on the winding road. Every so often he had to step on the breaks and steer the car into a lay-by to let another vehicle pass. Most of the roads on the island were single track ones. Occasionally Tom would glance her way, eyes twinkling, a smile on his lips. He was very good looking, Grace thought again, taking in his faded jeans and jumper combo.

They had gone for a drink in the evening after the boat ride. Grace was used to antagonising about what to wear as the places Paul usually took her to were classy and expensive. Tom on the other hand, had suggested the local pub. Grace had a suspicion it was the only establishment nearby and they had met at the Black Cow, Johnny behind the bar, giving them a friendly and warm welcome.

In the end Grace had thrown on a pair of jeans, a cashmere jumper and her heeled boots. It felt refreshing to not spend an eternity rifling through her wardrobe, trying to find an outfit that was just right. Instead she had felt comfortable in her clothes, soaking up the cosy atmosphere of the pub. They had ordered local beer and the conversation had been easy, uncomplicated. Any worries Grace might have had about stilted conversations or feeling bored vanished within the first few minutes. Tom was good company and easy to be around. He seemed very grounded and at peace with himself. He had a great sense of humour and amused her with stories of island life. He made her feel at ease which allowed her to relax and be herself. Tom didn't seem to expect anything from her, he simply seemed happy to be in her company.

Drinks had turned into dinner and Tom had offered to show her the island. Grace had hesitated. She was here to help Josie after all. She couldn't just take off with someone she barely knew, could she? And besides, she might have left Paul in a physical sense but she wasn't officially free. They had yet to end their relationship.

In the letter she had left Paul, she had merely asked for time. It had felt cruel and cowardly to end a relationship of five years via letter rather than face to face.

After voicing her concerns about Josie, Tom had simply said, 'Bring her along, the more the merrier.' They had eventually agreed to visit Duart Castle on Tom's next free day.

When Grace had told Josie, she had merely laughed.

'My dear child,' she had said, 'you go and have fun. I'm too old to play gooseberry, besides I have things to do. Look at this place!'

'But I should help you with that,' Grace had protested.

'Should you?' Josie's eyes had mustered her shrewdly. 'I thought all the "shoulds", were the very thing you were trying to get away from?'

And so here she was with Tom on her way to Duart Castle. It was a cool day but the wind had dropped and every now and again the weak sunlight burst through the clouds. Most importantly though, it wasn't raining. Tom turned off the main road onto a stony path with a grass verge running through the middle. Trees lined either side until suddenly they gave way to a bay. The sea glinted a deep blue grey and in the distance Duart Castle, with its thick walls, stood proudly, dominating the water between the island and the mainland. It was a stunning view and Grace couldn't stop taking it all in.

'Did I promise too much?' Tom joked, his mouth turned into a wide smile.

'It's a tad underwhelming,' Grace joked back and they burst into laughter.

Ever one to be prepared, Grace had tried to read up on the castle on the internet, however, the internet coverage on the island was patchy at best so her research capabilities had been limited. She knew that the castle was very old, built in the fourteenth century and she had read that in the eighteenth century it had become a ruin and had only been restored in 1911.

Tom parked the car and they purchased their entry tickets at a little booth just outside the castle. Grace took in the sweeping views and then turned to the imposing entry way of the castle. They declined a guided tour, opting instead to look around the castle and grounds at their own pace. Grace loved old buildings. She always felt a shiver of excitement when she thought about the people that had lived there before, their histories, their lives, what they might have experienced and what fate awaited them.

As they moved from room to room, Tom took her hand. Grace tensed for a moment and then relaxed. It felt nice to be holding hands, comforting somehow, a sign to the outside world that she belonged with someone.

After they had perused the rooms and displays at their leisure, Tom suggested to climb up to the top of the tower that provided visitors with a viewing platform. After climbing endless stairs, Grace had to stop for a moment when they emerged onto the platform to catch her breath. God, she was so unfit! It was cold up here but the view was even more stunning than from below. You could see for miles!

'Wow,' Grace breathed.

'Wow indeed,' Tom echoed and Grace turned to find him looking at her. A shiver ran down her spine, not altogether unpleasantly. Tom came closer and brushed a strand of her hair behind her ear. The gesture was intimate, tender, like he might have done this with her hair a million times before.

What are you doing? a voice inside her demanded. *You can't do this!*

Tom looked into her eyes, his green ones meeting her blue ones, before he touched his lips to hers. Butterflies took flight in her stomach as she returned his kiss. When they came apart, they smiled at each other, bright, luminous smiles.

Actually, I think I can, Grace told the critical voice inside her.

Tom took her hand and drew her to him whilst he lifted his phone with the other.

'I think this calls for a celebratory selfie, don't you?' he winked at her before pressing the button. Grace would treasure that photo of two youngish people, genuine smiles on their faces, happy to be in each other's company, happy to be alive. For her it captured a moment when she felt able to silence her inner critic and listened to her own instincts. It captured a moment of freedom.

*

Before leaving the castle grounds, Tom and Grace stopped by the café for strong coffee and an excellent, spicy tomato soup. Grace relished the warmth that was winding its way through her cold bones but she wondered afterwards whether that warmth had more to do with Tom than with the delicious soup. His green eyes twinkled and his mouth seemed to permanently smile at her and they had an easy way of being together. Their conversations felt natural and the flirting felt nice, exciting even.

Grace couldn't remember the last time she felt excited in Paul's presence. She pushed the thought away. She didn't want to think about Paul right now. Before the drive home, they kissed some more in the car and Grace could feel her heart racing as their kisses became more urgent, more passionate. Reluctantly she pulled away and smoothed down her hair.

'As much as I like kissing you,' she said, 'and I really do, I don't think your car is the best place to go to second base in.' She had meant it as a joke and to her relief Tom laughed.

'Don't knock it 'til you've tried it,' he joked back. 'I suppose the lady requires more appropriate and lavish quarters.'

'Yes indeed, the lady does. But right now the lady requires you to drive her back to her humble abode.' Grace glanced out of the window. 'It's getting late and I don't want Josie to get worried.'

'No problem,' Tom replied. 'Let's get going.'

They were quiet on the drive home, each lost in their own thoughts. Grace couldn't help but feel guilty as her conscience kicked in with a vengeance. What was she doing kissing another man when she was still technically in a relationship? And even if she wasn't, she didn't come here to find another man but to find herself. Wasn't that the whole point of why she decided to leave?

But was it really so bad? She liked Tom, he made her feel things she hadn't felt in a very long time. And wasn't she trusting her instincts? Was it so wrong to kiss him? Was it so wrong to pursue what made her happy? The battle raged on in Grace's head, her fingers nervously twisting in her lap.

Before she knew it, Tom steered the Land Rover over the gravelly lane and pulled up outside the house.

'Here we are,' he said, 'back safe and sound.' He smiled at her.

'Tom, there is something you need to know,' Grace said. She needed to tell him, he deserved to know. She didn't want him to think she was just toying with him.

Tom leaned over and put a finger on her lips. 'Not today,' he whispered. 'Today was a perfect day and I want to remember it this way.' He kissed her deeply and she clung to him, enjoying her nerve endings fizzing into life. Tom touched his forehead to hers.

'I'd better get going otherwise we are not getting out of this car. Whatever you need to tell me, tell me next time, ok?'

Grace nodded.

'Next time,' she echoed.

'I'll call you tomorrow,' he said as Grace climbed out of the car. Grace waved as Tom drove down the lane again, the Land Rover vanishing into the darkness. Grace looked up at the sky, a thousand stars twinkling back at her.

Oh boy, she thought. *What have I got myself into?!*

As she unlocked the heavy front door, she realised that she didn't just like Tom, she *really* liked him, adding another complication to an already complicated endeavour.

Owen

I smile. At least I think I can still smile. I'd like to think so. Josie is holding onto her coffee cup for dear life, her eyes darting around the kitchen as if I was hiding somewhere.

In actual fact I'm right in front of her but expecting her to see me was probably pushing the boat out. I'm amazed that she can hear me. I didn't think that saying the words out loud would work.

She has grown older, of course she has. There are new lines across her forehead, around her eyes and lips. Her hair has gone white and she is no longer as skinny as she was back then. But those eyes still hold the same energy and fire they always had, albeit no longer on full blast. She looks more weary now, a bit run down, tired. But I know from watching her these last few days that she doesn't sleep well. She's troubled, tossing and turning in bed, staring at the ceiling, thoughts racing across her mind.

My heart, if I still have one, feels fit for bursting. I still love her with the same fierce passion I always felt for her. With that realisation, sadness washes over me. I would be here with her now. We would have grown old together, I know it.

With the sadness, the familiar waves of anger sweep over me.

Why did I have to die?

Why was I driving too fast?

Why was I such an idiot?

I try to control my emotions. These questions have been plaguing me for an eternity and there is no answer to them and no way to change what has happened.

A startling realisation comes to me, seemingly out of nowhere. Just as Josie has been holding on to me, I have been holding on to those questions. They have kept me tethered, unable to move, paralysed by the wish to get a second chance, to be alive again, to make different choices.

I sigh. I have been on my own for a long time. Which brings me to another question.

'Where were you all this time? Why didn't you come back sooner?'

Josie startles again, looking around her. I can see she is trying to stay calm, probably questioning whether she has lost her mind.

'Is that really you?' she asks.

I nod, before realising that she cannot see me and even if she could, I'm no longer sure what I actually look like.

'Yes,' I reply, 'it's really me.'

'Wow,' she whispers and I can see tears glistening in her eyes. 'How is that possible?'

'I don't know,' I say. 'All I know is that I have been waiting here a long time. Where were you?'

My tone has a bitterness to it that I wish I could take out, but the truth is that I do feel bitter. And abandoned. Josie leans back in her chair, wiping over her eyes, reaching for the coffee cup in front of her, no doubt wishing it held something stronger than coffee. She takes a deep breath.

'I'm so sorry, Owen,' she says.

Her voice is quiet, filled with emotions I cannot immediately ascertain.

'I guess it was just too painful. Coming here after you died.' She pauses. 'You are still dead?'

'Yes,' I reply. 'I don't know what form I now have but I guess I've been haunting this joint, waiting for you.'

She smiles. As she continues talking, the smile fades.

'I don't know what to say. I just couldn't face it. I wasn't strong enough. This place,' she gestures at the house, 'it was so filled with us. Our plans, our dreams, our future together. But all that was gone the night you died. Losing you broke me.'

She is crying now, wiping frantically at her eyes. I want to reach out to her, to fold her in my arms, to tell her that everything will be ok. I curse my non-existent body. All these years I took it for granted and now I'd do anything to have it back, to be able to feel touch, to feel physically present.

'It's ok, Josie,' I say instead. 'I understand. You're here now. That's all that matters.'

For some reason this makes her cry harder.

'Oh God,' she sobs. 'I missed you so much, Owen.'

Suddenly a bark fills the room. Biscuit has sauntered in, sniffing the air, his fur standing up in tufts. They did always say that dogs could sense ghosts.

'It's all right,' I say. 'I'm not trying to hurt you or Josie.'

Josie looks up and beckons Biscuit to her, burying her face in his fur and mumbling nonsense to him. Biscuit plants himself next to her chair and after a while Josie is able to compose herself.

'Owen?' she asks.

'Yes?'

'What's it like to be a ghost?'

'Crap,' I answer and she laughs. God, I have missed that laugh.

'Ok,' she chuckles. 'What do we do now? Surely, you can't be a ghost forever. It's not right. You should be at peace.' Tears glisten again.

'Peace sounds nice,' I answer and suddenly I feel bone tired. It really does take it out of you communicating with the living.

'Let's think about it,' I say, my voice quiet. 'We can talk about it later.'

I close my eyes and darkness claims me.

Josephine (Josie) –Now

Josie walked along the beach, wind tearing at the tendrils of her hair escaping her beanie hat. Biscuit was running in front of her, his legs stretching as he raced across the sand. Josie looked out at the waves, letting the colour of the ocean imprint on her mind.

She couldn't believe that she talked to Owen! To hear his voice again after all this time felt like a precious gift. She didn't know how or why but she didn't care. Owen had come back to her and that was all that mattered.

For the first time in a very long while, she felt light, her heart no longer heavy, chained by the weight of grief. She felt able to breathe.

She felt energised.

She felt alive.

Everything seemed to make sense again. Her life only ever had meaning with Owen in it. She stopped in her tracks. No, that wasn't quite true. And it would not be fair to pile all of that responsibility on Owen's shoulders. She might not have fully lived since his death but she has had meaningful conversations, she's laughed and she had Biscuit. And lately, she also found meaning in her friendship with Grace.

She continued walking, her mood no longer euphoric but pensive. Owen had been stuck in that house waiting for her.

But why? Unfinished business, wasn't that what everyone said about ghosts? Perhaps it was because they loved each other so much, maybe too much.

She thought back to their time together. They had spent all their time with each other, they had been inseparable, perhaps to the extent that left little room for other people. And yet they had also often argued, both of them stubborn, and Josie was no wall flower back then. She knew her own mind and wasn't afraid to speak it.

As the years went by, she learned tactfulness and her temper became calmer with age and experience. Suddenly not every battle felt important, some things she was able to just let go without spending so much energy on fighting them. She would like to think she had become wiser as she got older. She smiled. Didn't everyone?

She wondered what Owen would look like now? And would they have stayed together? Would theirs have been a love story that you didn't hear very often anymore? The exception to the rule of break ups and divorce?

She had no way of knowing. Josie watched Biscuit for a few moments, who was racing after a seagull, jumping up and barking.

One thing she wanted for Owen after he died was for him to be at peace. She had prayed for that and it had given her comfort on many dark and sleepless nights. The fact that he had been roaming the house upset her deeply. Josie sighed and dug her hands into the pockets of her coat. She would love to think that she could spend time with Owen now, talking to him, having him back in her life in this very unusual way.

But deep down she knew that this wasn't right. He hadn't been waiting all this time for them to simply chat and continue where they had left off. Her alive and kicking and him nothing but a voice in the emptiness of a room, trapped in limbo land. He had been waiting for peace. And she was the one that could give him that. She was the one he had been waiting for. Josie stared into the wind, the waves crashing onto the shore.

She was the one to set him free.

Chapter 7

Grace

Grace was staring out of the window, watching the rolling waves and the grey expanse of sky above them. Somehow it suited her mood. The ocean seemed restless today much like herself. She had tossed and turned all night, unable to sleep, unable to find a solution to her dilemma without anyone getting hurt. It had been a mistake to go on that day trip with Tom. And yet she couldn't quite bring herself to regret it.

Now, a few days later, she was sitting in the window seat in the living room, a steaming mug of coffee beside her, a book lying open in her lap, the page unread.

Walking away from her life was meant to make things simpler and now she found things to be even more complicated. Her mind told her that she couldn't pursue whatever was between her and Tom because she wasn't technically free to do so. But her heart was saying that this might be part of her journey, to discover who she really was, and they were all adults after all. She wasn't about to marry Tom, for crying out loud.

Josie had been sitting quietly in an armchair, concentrating on a crossword puzzle. Biscuit was lying by her feet and snoozing.

'Penny for them?' Josie asked after a while.

The question startled Grace out of her reverie.

'I'm not sure it's all that interesting,' she replied, turning away from the window and facing Josie. Josie looked back at her with inquisitive eyes that missed nothing. She was wearing woollen trousers and a forest green long jumper, accessorised with a couple of beaded necklaces. She looked, Grace thought, effortlessly chic.

'My dear girl,' Josie said, 'you have been staring out of that window until the cows come home. Has something happened with Tom?'

Grace shook her head. 'No, Tom is lovely ...' she didn't finish the sentence.

'But?' Josie prompted.

'It's just that technically I'm still with Paul. You see we never officially broke up. And it's not fair to either of them is it, if I start something with Tom when I'm not really free to do so.'

'I see,' said Josie. 'Do you still love Paul?'

Grace sighed and put her head in her hands.

'I don't know,' she admitted. 'Paul and I have been together for a long time but for some time now I have felt stifled in the relationship. Paul likes doing things a certain way and there doesn't really seem room for any spontaneity or for new things. And I guess I've always been ok with that because I'm not really, you know, adventurous or anything like that, and it felt safe and I suppose easier to just go along with what Paul wanted. I always thought he had my best interests at heart but now I'm not so sure anymore.'

'And how did you feel in Tom's company?' Josie asked.

Grace took a moment to consider the question. 'Relaxed. I feel like I can be myself and we get on really well. He is easy to be around. But I've only known him for five minutes; it's not really fair to compare the two like that is it?'

'We're not comparing the two though are we?' Josie challenged. 'We're merely discussing how you feel in their presence.'

'I suppose so,' Grace conceded. 'This just all feels so complicated.' She sighed, feeling frustrated.

'It sounds to me like Tom is perhaps easy to be around because the two of you have just met and there is no history there. You're getting to know each other and that's always exciting. And you already feel relaxed in his presence. Whereas with Paul you have identified that there are things you are no longer happy with. Maybe you need to decide whether those are deal breakers or whether there is still enough left that makes the relationship worth salvaging. Perhaps you've outgrown it?'

Grace smiled. 'You would have made a great therapist.'

Josie laughed. 'Wisdom comes with age, my dear, and making a great many mistakes along the way.'

'How did you know that Owen was the one for you?'

'He made me laugh and he kept making me laugh.'

Grace nodded. She had laughed a lot with Tom during the time they spent together this week but she couldn't remember the last time she and Paul had laughed at something together.

'Did you have any regrets?' Grace asked.

Josie's eyes softened. 'Oh sweetheart,' she replied, 'we all have regrets.'

Grace thought about this and then made a decision. She needed to talk to Paul, the sooner the better. And then she would talk to Tom.

'Would you excuse me, Josie? I'm going to try and find some signal. I've got a couple of phone calls to make.'

'No problem,' Josie replied and smiled as Grace left the room.

*

In the hallway, Grace pulled on her walking boots and grabbed her raincoat. Phone signal was patchy at the best of times but she had found a spot in the garden that promised a whole two bars which should be enough to make a phone call. The wind whipped at her hair and she took deep breaths. She hadn't spoken to Paul for a few weeks now, mainly because she had her phone turned off and avoided her social media prior to coming to the island. She wondered whether he would be glad or angry to hear from her.

Only one way to find out. Grace dialled the number and waited, her anxiety making her heart race. After three rings, Paul answered the phone.

'Hello?'

'Paul, it's Grace.'

Silence.

'Can you talk? Or are you busy right now?'

'No, I can talk, at least for a few minutes. How are you? It's good to hear your voice.'

'I'm ok, how are you?'

'How the hell do you think I am?' Paul exploded. 'You've

gone awol? and I've been worried sick about you. Where are you? And why haven't you called?'

Grace took a deep breath. Anger it was then.

'I've not gone awol. I wrote you a letter and I sent that text a few weeks ago to let you know I'm fine.'

'Grace, you just up and leave and I'm supposed to just say oh that's ok because you wrote me a letter? It's not acceptable. Your parents are worried too.'

Grace sighed at the mention of her parents. She should have known that Paul would contact them. She swallowed her irritation.

'I just needed some space. I need to figure out what I want from my life.'

'Are you having a breakdown? It sure sounds like one'

'How would you know? Look, I'm just telling you how I feel.'

'And I'm telling you this isn't you, Grace. Where are you?'

'I'm on the Isle of Mull. Scotland.'

There was a pause on the other end of the phone.

'Wow. You really did want to get away, huh?!'

'Paul, please believe me when I say I am fine, really.'

'When are you coming back?'

'I don't know.'

'And what about us? Are we over?'

'I don't know.'

Silence.

'Why don't you write me another damn letter when you do know,' Paul said and put down the phone.

Josephine (Josie) – Now

Josie made herself another cup of coffee and settled back down in her armchair. She looked out of the window that moments ago Grace had stared out of, lost in thought.

Since coming back to the island, Josie found herself reflecting on Owen's death and on why it had not only devastated but annihilated her, so that all she could do was merely exist. Perhaps it was because she had not only loved Owen but he had been her everything, her family, her rock. And he had seen her for who she truly was.

Sure, she had had a lot of friends who had loved her. They had loved her sense of humour, her independence, her fierceness in the face of problems or obstacles.

But Owen, Owen had been able to see through all of that to her core. He had seen the desperately lonely girl who tried so hard to hide her vulnerability.

It struck her now that with his death, she had gone back to hiding that vulnerability, the truth and depth of her feelings, perhaps even from herself. She had shut herself off from everyone, had kept her friends at arm's length. And with the years going by, friends had stopped calling and she had burrowed further and further into an existence that left her not only on the outside of things but also lonelier than ever. Renting out her rooms on a short term basis, keeping her distance from her guests, letting no one in. She had thought she was protecting herself. She couldn't bear to get hurt again. In reality she had been nothing but hurting.

Josie took a sip of coffee, cradling the warm mug in her hands. And then Grace had come along. Josie smiled as she thought back to their first meeting. This young woman with a suitcase full of problems and questions had slowly nudged her to reconnect with life, and to her surprise Josie had let her.

She was grateful though, and whilst her grief threatened to overwhelm her on some days, she also felt great relief in allowing it out in the open. And if she was honest with herself, she could think of no better place in which to allow herself to slowly heal than this island that she loved almost as much as she loved Owen.

Grace

Grace had gone for a long walk afterwards, letting the sea calm her turmoil and the wind toy with her hair. She felt bad that she was hurting Paul and worrying her parents. She didn't mean to cause anyone any pain. But she was in pain too, why did nobody seem to notice that?

Question upon question raced through her restless mind. What did she want? Where did she go from here? Should she cut all ties to Paul or should she go back to a relationship she may or may not be completely happy in? Did she feel Paul met some of her needs?

Should he have to? Shouldn't love be enough?

And what about her work? She handed in her notice and she did not feel any regret about that. It had been the right thing to do.

But what now? She had to return to work at some point. Should she go back and simply start applying for a job at a different company? Wasn't that what she was trying to get away from? What actually was it that she was running from?

Question upon question and Grace didn't have the answers to any of them. She felt her heart racing with anxiety as an all too familiar panic grabbed hold of her.

Grace stopped then and looked around her. Looked at the sea and the waves, the rocks that glistened purple when the sun shone, the grass underneath her feet, the sky above, so vast, today a greyish blue. Slowly her breathing returned to normal.

Grace decided to allow herself time to find the answers. She wouldn't spend her days overanalysing everything because she felt she would become lost in the pros and cons of the situation. Perhaps if she simply allowed the answers to find her, perhaps then she would come to some conclusions. Her very basic needs were covered. She had some savings to tide her over and at the moment she was staying with Josie.

Josie had not told her how long she planned to stay on Mull and that suited her just fine, after all this was a beautiful place to be in.

Grace also decided to send her parents a message, reassuring them that she was ok and not to worry.

Decisions made, Grace returned to the house with a renewed sense of determination. Right now she didn't know what she wanted to do about her relationship with Paul or work or Tom for that matter.

But maybe that was ok. Maybe for now it was ok not to know. One thing she did know was that she wanted a hot shower and a cup of sugary tea.

After all, wasn't a cup of tea the answer to everything?!

Josephine (Josie) – Now

Josie looked up at the jaunty sign above 'the Book Shed, and fingered her necklace nervously. Johnny had told her it would do her good to do a bit of volunteer work whilst she was here.

'Something to keep your mind occupied,' he had said, concern etched into his weathered face. Josie had pulled a face.

'Besides, you're good with people,' he had added and Josie had relented, knowing that when Johnny had set his mind on something, he was as stubborn as a mule.

Greta, the woman who ran the Book Shed, had been happy for Josie to volunteer for a few hours a week. She had sounded around Josie's age on the phone, friendly and upbeat, although the line had been bad and crackling, the phone signal as ever intermittent on the island.

There is nothing to feel nervous about, Josie told herself sternly before straightening her back and marching into the shop. A woman, presumably Greta, stood behind a wooden counter in a square, not very large room. The walls were lined with shelves, books in every available nook and cranny, a cheery bell over the door announcing Josie's arrival.

'You must be Josie, welcome,' Greta greeted her, a smile on her face. She came towards Josie, hand outstretched. 'I've heard so much about you. Johnny's an old friend,' she confided and Josie smiled.

'Johnny seems to be everyone's friend,' she replied and Greta laughed.

'It is a small island. Would you like a cup of tea before we get started? As you can see we're overrun with people.'

Josie laughed and said that a cup of tea would be lovely. She felt herself relax and her nerves dissipated. She liked Greta, liked her sense of humour, the way she poked fun at island life. Like Owen, she thought, and then pushed the thought away. She couldn't fall apart on her first day on the job.

Cup of tea in hand, Greta explained that they mainly sold second-hand books. She talked Josie through the payment system and how to keep check of the stock.

'I hope you're not looking for excitement or being run off your feet. We're not very busy most of the time. The locals mainly bop in for a bit of a chat and in season tourists come to find a good beach read. Now and then someone might look for a recommendation.'

Josie, who was an avid reader herself, nodded enthusiastically.

'Not a problem,' she said.

'Great, then I think you're all set. We'll do today together and then next time you'll be on your own. I'm really glad you called, you know.'

'Why's that?'

'You doing a few hours means I can spend a bit more time on my new hobby. I've started doing my family tree. It's fascinating, you never know what you might stumble upon and before you know it three hours have gone,' Greta said and laughed. 'Besides,' she placed a warm hand on Josie's arm, 'from what Johnny told me, it sounds like you could use a bit of a distraction. It must be hard being back here after all this time. Not that he told me all that much, please don't think that,' she rushed on.

Josie smiled and reassured Greta.

'Don't worry, I know what he's like. And you're right, it is hard.' She took a deep breath. 'So thank you.'

They smiled at each other.

'Now then, do you mind if I have a look at what you've got on the shelves so I know what to recommend to the locals?'

'Knock yourself out,' Greta replied and went to put the kettle on.

Grace

Grace was pulling on her jacket to take Biscuit for a walk when her mobile rang, startling her. She had almost forgotten her ringtone due to the intermittent phone signal.

Her parents. For a split second Grace thought about letting the phone go to voicemail but then decided it might be better to take the call.

'Hello?' she said, swiping to answer the call.

'Grace, darling, how are you?'

'Hi, Mum, I'm good. I'm just about to take Josie's dog for a walk.' Biscuit looked up at her expectantly as if he understood every word. She stroked his head, smiling at him fondly.

'Is Josie the woman you're staying with?' Grace had mentioned Josie in her message to her parents that she sent a couple of days ago, reassuring them that she was ok.

'Yes,' she replied. 'How are you, Mum?'

'Darling, we're worried. When are you coming home?'

'I don't know, Mum. I'm figuring things out. But you don't have to worry. I'm ok.'

'But Paul said that you seem to be having some sort of breakdown. He phoned yesterday, he was in a right state, the poor thing.'

'I left Paul a letter explaining things and I talked to him the other day. I'm not having a breakdown, I just need some time to think things through, you know, what I want from my life.'

'Darling, what are you talking about? You have everything, and Paul is a catch, you two could get married, have children. Isn't that what you want?'

Grace sighed. She should have known her mother would find it difficult to understand where Grace was at. To most people Paul was a catch. She had thought so too, hadn't she?

Grace heard another voice in the background.

'Is that her? Give me the phone, Emilia!'

'Grace? Grace?' her father's voice boomed into her ear.

'Hello, Dad,' Grace answered.

'Grace, what is all this nonsense I keep hearing about? And since when don't you answer your phone? Your mother has been worried sick!'

'I'm ok, Dad, really, there's no need to worry.'

'No need to worry, are you kidding me? What are you doing in bloody Scotland? Paul said you were having some sort of breakdown? What do you think you're playing at?'

She would kill Paul, Grace thought silently. Trust him to rile up her parents, especially her dad. Paul knew that Grace's relationship with her father wasn't always easy.

'I'm just figuring things out,' Grace said, feeling like she was repeating herself.

'What is there to figure out? You are coming home on the

next train. You and Paul will sort things out and then you can go back to work.'

Grace let out a sigh.

'Actually, Dad, I quit my job before I left.'

There was stunned silence on the other end of the phone.

'You did what? Grace, what has gotten into you? You're not thinking clearly. You are coming home this instant and we will sort this out. Get you some pills if necessary, half of Britain is taking antidepressants these days, though I haven't got the faintest idea what you could possibly be depressed about.'

Grace felt her pulse quicken and a knot tighten in her stomach. Trust her father to be unsympathetic.

'No,' Grace said, her voice quivering.

'What was that?'

'No,' Grace repeated, taking a deep breath, her voice firmer this time. 'I'm not coming home, Dad. I'm an adult.'

'You might well be an adult but you sure as hell aren't acting like one!'

'Why? Because I'm not dancing to your tune anymore?' Grace felt anger rush through her body. 'Well sorry to disappoint you, Dad, but I'm trying to find my own tune. Between you and Paul it's no wonder I've never been able to find my own voice.' Grace breathed heavily, running out of steam.

'Well if that's how you feel, make your own bed, Grace, but you will have to lie in it. Don't come crying to your mother and me when things go invariably wrong.'

Tears pricked Grace's eyes. Maybe she had been too harsh?

'Dad, please try to understand, I just—'

But her father had already disconnected the call.

Grace stared at her phone in disbelief, the tears now running freely down her cheeks. She had known that her parents wouldn't understand but she had hoped they would support her anyway.

Suddenly she felt very alone.

Without thinking twice about it, Grace made another call and five minutes later she rushed out of the door, having forgotten all about her planned walk with Biscuit whose sad eyes rested on the closed front door.

*

Tom lived in a small run down cottage, just outside Fionnphort. The cottage had seen better days but looked sturdy and for the most part intact. There was a small front garden that was mainly taken up by stacked lobster crates and bits of various machinery. A cheery garden gnome bid Grace a warm welcome which made her smile. Grace took a moment to collect herself before she knocked on the wooden front door. It didn't take long for Tom to answer.

'Hey,' he said, an easy smile on his lips. 'It's great to see you! Please come in.'

'Thanks,' Grace said, stepping into the hallway. The cottage was small with low ceilings and doors leading off the main hallway and a wooden staircase leading upstairs. Even though it seemed sparsely furnished, it exuded charm and character and Grace felt instantly at ease.

'Can I offer you a drink? How about a beer or glass of wine?'

'Wine please,' Grace replied as Tom gestured for her to go into the living room.

'Your wish is my command. Back in a sec. Do make yourself at home.'

Grace went to the living room window and looked out, even though there was not much to see as darkness was falling. She chewed her lip, turning back to look at the room. The log burner was crackling with a freshly built fire and some of the walls exposed the brickwork, giving the room a cosy quality. Tom had put in two squishy sofas which took up most of the space and a flat screen TV occupied one corner of the room. Even though Grace could tell that this was a bachelor pad, it did feel homely.

Tom returned with two glasses of red wine.

'Here you are,' he said, handing her one of the glasses. 'Cheers'

'Cheers,' Grace said, clinking her glass to his and taking a sip. The wine was delicious.

'I like your place,' she said.

'Thanks. It does need a bit of work and I keep meaning to do it but somehow never get round to it. When you've spent all day on the water with testy tourists, there are days when you just want to sit on the sofa and watch some mindless TV.' He gave her a sheepish grin.

Grace laughed. 'I can imagine.'

They sank onto one of said sofas.

'So,' Tom said, 'how are you doing? You sounded a bit upset on the phone.'

Grace took another sip of wine, taking her time to answer.

'I just spoke to my parents,' she said.

Tom watched her and nodded.

'Bad conversation?'

Grace nodded. 'You could say that.'

'Do you want to talk about it? I know you said the other day that you wanted to tell me something.'

'I know and I do need to tell you something,' Grace said, putting her wine glass onto the coffee table. 'But right now,' she continued, 'I don't really want to talk at all.'

She leaned forward, pulling Tom towards her and kissed him. Tom was initially surprised but then allowed himself to sink into the kiss.

'Is that ok with you?' Grace murmured.

Tom smiled against her lips. 'Fine by me, as long as you're sure?'

'I'm sure,' Grace said.

And then they didn't need to say anything at all.

Chapter 8

Grace

The morning light sneaked through the sunshine yellow curtains of Tom's bedroom. Grace blinked sleepily and stretched before feeling momentarily disorientated. She paused for a moment and became aware of Tom's breathing. She sighed. She really had to stop making a habit of sleeping in strangers' beds, although technically Tom wasn't a stranger.

Not anymore.

She smiled as images from last night danced across her inner eye. Maybe it had been a reckless thing to do because her relationship with Paul was still unresolved, but suddenly Grace found that she didn't care anymore. And then that awful phone call with her parents. Grace had felt that the people in her life didn't really know her at all and perhaps what was worse, didn't seem to want to hear what she was telling them. They had this view of her which seemed rigid and immobile.

Last night Grace wanted to be held and desired and Tom had been happy to oblige. She turned to look at him. His dark hair was dishevelled and he had one arm thrown over his head. He seemed totally relaxed. She was just about to snuggle up to him when her mobile phone started to ring.

Tom grunted and mumbled, turning over and pulling the duvet over his head.

'Sorry,' Grace said whilst fishing for her mobile phone and swiping to answer it.

'Grace?' The line crackled.

'Josie, hi! Is everything ok?'

'I could ask you the same thing,' Josie replied and chuckled.

Grace blushed. In her hurry yesterday she had completely forgotten to tell Josie she was going out. And poor Biscuit had also slipped her mind. She bit her lip.

'I'm so sorry. I had a phone call with my parents yesterday and afterwards I just needed to get out. But I should have let you know, I'm sorry.'

'Don't worry, love. I understand. Are you somewhere safe though?'

'Yes, I'm with Tom.'

'I thought as much. That's great news first thing in the morning though.'

Grace laughed.

'If you say so.'

'The reason I'm calling is that you have the car.'

Oh God, the car. Grace slapped her forehead. She had taken the car. She really had been a bit all over the place last night.

'Yes, I'm—'

'Before you apologise again,' Josie interrupted, 'which is of course totally unnecessary, would you be able to pick up some things from the shop in Bunessan? I have decided to set a date for scattering Owen's ashes.' There was a pause.

'It's time,' Josie said.

'Oh wow, Josie, that's big,' Grace faltered, unsure of what to say.

'I have to let him go. Owen deserves to be at peace.'

Grace considered this for a moment, thinking that this was an odd choice of words. But perhaps Josie didn't want to acknowledge yet that it was really her that needed to be at peace with her past.

'How about you text me what you need and then I meet you back at the house?'

'Sounds like a plan,' Josie replied.

'Great, I'll see you then.'

'Oh and Grace?'

'Yes?'

'There's no rush. Take your time.'

Grace could practically see the twinkle in Josie's eyes and blushed again as she hung up the phone.

'Is everything ok?' Tom asked sleepily.

'Yes, everything's fine. Josie just needs me to pick up some things from the village. She has decided on a date to scatter Owen's ashes.'

'Wow, that's kind of a big deal.'

'Yes it is. I hope it will bring her some closure or peace at least.'

'Possibly.'

There was silence as they both thought of Josie. Grace had told Tom about Owen and the reason she and Josie had come to Mull. He had been empathic and understanding and didn't press Grace further on any details. She had liked him even more then.

'Anyways, how did you sleep in my humble abode?' Tom changed the subject.

'Great thanks. How about you?'

'I must still be dreaming because you stayed the night.'

Grace laughed and batted Tom with her pillow.

'You're terrible,' she said but she could feel herself blushing again.

'But the best kind of terrible,' he replied, pulling her to him and kissing her.

'Yes, definitely the best kind,' she murmured.

*

After making love again, Grace and Tom shared a breakfast of eggs, bacon and strong black coffee before Grace got back into Josie's car and drove towards Bunessan. The morning light shimmered on the ocean, making the water look like a glittering expanse of blue and turquoise and Grace glanced at it every so often as she negotiated the curvy road. She was lost in her thoughts and as she rounded a corner, she had to suddenly press the brake pedal, the car coming to an emergency stop, lurching Grace forwards towards the windshield. Her heart hammering loudly in her chest, adrenaline pumping through her, Grace peeled her face from the windscreen and looked straight into the eyes of a Scottish Highland cow, who was giving her a look that might have said, 'What the hell, woman, I'm grazing here!'

Five of those majestic animals were in the middle of the road, munching away the grass that lined the verge. Grace looked around her but there was not another soul in sight.

She sat back in the car seat and suddenly burst into laughter. *How fabulous,* she thought. Cows in the road. She smiled. She was used to heavy traffic and roadworks but she had to admit she preferred the cows!

She loved this island, she suddenly realised. She carefully edged the Mini forwards and manoeuvred around the animals before continuing on her way.

Grace couldn't wipe the smile off her face and as she turned up the radio to some cheerful tune, she marvelled at how happy she felt here, on this island, in the middle of nowhere, sleeping with a guy she barely knew. If she didn't know better, she would hardly recognise herself.

But the fact was that she felt good.

Happy. For the first time in a long time.

And right now that was good enough for her.

Grace parked the car in the car park overlooking the water and watched two seagulls racing each other across the sky, their calls loud and piercing. She scanned over the list Josie had sent her earlier. As she got out of the car, she took a moment to drink in the scenery and letting the ocean breeze wash over her. The sea was calm today and there were only a few clouds scattered across the sky, but the temperature was cold.

Grace walked towards the village shop which was half the size of most supermarkets in England. The woman behind the till smiled at Grace as she entered, wishing her a good morning. She was wearing a padded gilet and fingerless gloves to protect her from the morning chill as the door remained wide open. It didn't take Grace long to make her rounds through the supermarket and pick up most of the items. The rest she would have to get at the big supermarket in Craignure. Perhaps she could make the trip tomorrow as it was located in the other direction. Grace hadn't asked Josie when she had set the date for but she assumed it wouldn't be tomorrow.

As she was driving back to the house, her phone rang again. Glancing at it quickly, Grace noticed that Josie had called twice. Maybe she had forgotten something? No matter. Grace would be at the house soon and she could always get what Josie had forgotten tomorrow when she drove to the bigger supermarket. Maybe she could meet Tom for a bite to eat at lunchtime if he wasn't working. He had already texted her, saying that he had had a great time with a smiley face and a heart emoji.

As Grace pulled up in front of the house, she noticed a big black SUV that hadn't been there before. Maybe Josie had visitors? Grabbing her things, Grace pushed open the front door.

'I'm back,' she called, unloading her shopping bags onto the flagstone floor and shutting the front door with her foot.

'I tried to call you,' Josie said, coming towards her, concern etched onto her face.

'I was driving,' Grace explained. 'Why, has something happened?'

'You have a visitor,' Josie said, pointing Grace towards the living room and squeezing her hand.

Dread settled in Grace's stomach as her mind raced as to who would have made the trip all the way up here to see her.

But there was only one person she could think of.

'Hello, Grace,' Paul said as she stepped into the lounge.

Owen

It's the middle of the night and the sky is an inky black dotted with twinkling stars like diamonds spilled onto black velvet. I'm in Josie's bedroom, watching her sleep, or not sleep might be more accurate. I don't think she senses I'm here; her mind seems to be elsewhere.

Biscuit lies sprawled out on the bottom of the bed, his eyes watching the darkness. I think he knows I'm here but he doesn't seem to mind.

I know she has decided to scatter my ashes. I overheard her speaking to Grace. She seems nice and I smile, thinking that Josie has always had a tendency to take the troubled under her wing.

But I'm worried. Not about me. Logic dictates that when my ashes are scattered, I might disappear completely, but to tell you the truth that might be a relief. I don't care for this semi-existence. It's lonely and even though I can now communicate with Josie, it's more painful than I expected.

It reminds me of what I have lost. It reminds me of everything I can never get back.

I am worried about Josie. She is not at peace either and by the looks of it she hasn't been for a long time. Perhaps scattering my ashes will bring us both peace and perhaps it will allow Josie to move forwards.

'Why didn't you have children?' I ask into the darkness.

Josie startles and I see her swivelling her head around, scanning the darkness before leaning back into her pillows.

'Owen?' she asks and then laughs self-consciously. 'Who else?' she says, answering her own question.

'You always wanted children,' I prompt, 'if I remember correctly you said you wanted a houseful.'

'With you,' she says after a while. 'I wanted a houseful of children with you. After you—' she clears her throat, 'after you died, I never met anyone else. Don't get me wrong, there were dalliances but nothing ever came close to what we had and I just couldn't see myself having children with anyone else. So I didn't.'

Her words make me feel so sad. Josie was so full of life and determination. It troubles me deeply to think that those things might have died with me. I choose my next words carefully. I don't want to hurt Josie but at the same time I have a feeling we are running out of time.

'What has happened to you?' I ask.

'Whatever do you mean?' she asks back.

'You used to be full of passion for life. You used to light up a room every time you walked into one. You were so determined to live life to the full on your terms, doing what you felt was important. That's why we took on this place, wasn't it? To do our own thing, be our own boss, the captain of our own destiny? And now, you seem, I don't know, diminished somehow. Faded. Like the spark has gone out.' I stop, exhausted suddenly.

'You died, Owen!' Josie explodes, her anger palpable. Biscuit jumps up and Josie strokes his head absentmindedly. 'You left me! Without you none of it seemed possible anymore.'

'So your answer was to hide away?' I ask after a moment.

'My answer was to somehow survive. Which is what I did. I'm sorry if this doesn't fit with the idealised version you have of me.'

'I'm glad to see there's still fire inside you,' I quip.

'Owen, you're an ass,' Josie exclaims and I laugh.

'Listen,' I say after a while. 'Just think about what I'm about to say. Don't argue with me, don't be angry, just think about it, ok? Promise me!'

'Fine,' Josie says, 'I promise, but only because of our circumstances,' she adds. I smile before I remember she can't see me. I remain silent for a moment, gathering my thoughts.

'Life is short, Josie,' I begin, which is a bit of a no-brainer really given that I am a ghost and all. 'You were the love of my life and I know you. I know the wonderful person you are. I know you have a beautiful soul and you are the bravest person I've ever known. So I want to say to you, stop hiding, stop running. You have so much more to give and the world is a better place because you're in it. Just look at what you're doing for Grace. Yes we had plans and yes things didn't work out how we hoped and me dying was a bit of a blow—'

'That's the understatement of the century, Owen,' Josie interrupts.

'Hey,' I say, 'you promised not to interrupt.'

'Sorry,' she replies, her arms crossed, 'do continue.'

'There is still time, Josie. And life is difficult. It's so very difficult at times, believe me, I know, I understand. It's a pain in the backside but do you know what's worse? Dying with regrets because you were too scared to take chances. I believe in you, Josie. I have always believed in you. We had plans for this place, remember? It was going to mean something.' I run out of steam and stop.

Josie is quiet for a long time, so long in fact that I wonder whether she has gone to sleep. That would just be my luck, making a heartfelt speech that sends the love of my life to sleep. I sigh.

'I'll think about it, Owen,' she eventually says into the silence, barely audible, but I hear her.

That is good enough for me.

Grace

Grace turned over in bed and scrunched up the pillow below her head. The room was pitch black and Grace usually slept like a baby since she and Josie had arrived on Mull. But tonight, her mind was racing and she kept tossing and turning. Paul's visit had unsettled her more than she liked to admit. It was true what they said, you can run but you can't hide. Grace sighed, her mind reliving her conversation with Paul.

She had stared at Paul before finding her voice. 'What are you doing here?'

'Hello to you too,' Paul had replied.

He looks good, Grace had thought. Clean shaven and immaculately dressed, but come to think of it that was what Paul always looked like; even when he felt stressed or upset about something you wouldn't know it by looking at him.

'To answer your question,' he said, 'I came here to see you and I suppose to talk some sense into you.'

Grace had bristled at his words and had forced herself to remain calm. If she started shouting now, she would only play into his view that she was having some sort of breakdown. Grace had sat down on the sofa, trying to calm her breathing. Paul had chosen an armchair opposite. He had looked around the living room, taking in the furniture and the views over the ocean.

'It's a nice place,' he had said.

'How did you even find me?' It had occurred to Grace that she hadn't left an address, and though she had told Paul she was on the Isle of Mull, she hadn't specified where exactly.

Paul had shrugged off her questions.

'It's a small island,' he had said, 'it wasn't that difficult. Besides, your friend, Josephine is it? She's well known in these parts. She seems nice.'

'She is nice.'

Paul had regarded her for a moment before leaning forward in his chair.

'Let's cut to the chase, Grace, ok? What is going on with you? What are you even doing here?' He hadn't left time for Grace to answer before continuing. 'We have a good life together. Good jobs, a nice house, we have plans for the future, for crying out loud. And all of a sudden you just walk out like none of it means anything? I'm sorry but it's not like you and just so you know your parents agree with me.'

Go figure, Grace had thought. It hadn't surprised her that Paul had gotten her parents involved. They had probably dissected the call she had had with them yesterday.

Paul probably saw himself in the role of the rescuer coming all this way to bring her home like the hero he thought he was.

'It's good of you to come all this way, Paul,' she had

replied, 'but there was really no need.' Paul went to protest but Grace had held up a hand.

'Let me finish,' she had said. 'You said I didn't give you an explanation but I did write you a letter and I did tell you where I was. I suppose that neither you or my parents want to hear what I am saying. Yes we have a good life together but whose life is it really? I feel like I had no say in it. You made all the decisions—'

'Because you like it that way,' Paul burst out.

'I did and I guess that's because all my life I have always done what other people expected of me. I've always been a people pleaser. But it no longer feels right.'

'It no longer feels right? What does that even mean? You act like I forced our life on you, like you didn't actively participate in it. But you did, Grace, and we were happy, weren't we?'

Paul's eyes had been pleading. Grace had sighed, bracing herself for what she was about to say. She had taken a deep breath and taken the plunge.

'I'm not happy anymore, Paul. And yes you are right. I did participate by allowing you to make all of the decisions in our relationship. But that is no longer ok for me. I am beginning to realise that I need to find my own voice, to live my life instead of everyone else's. You and my parents might think I have lost my mind but I feel the opposite, I feel like I've finally found it.' She had exhaled, slowly, trying to ignore the churning in her stomach.

Paul had been quiet for a moment, regarding her silently. She forced herself to maintain eye contact.

'So what does that mean for us, Grace? Are you just going

to throw away the last five years? What about the plans we had? Marriage, children?'

'I don't know if I want those things anymore, Paul.'

Paul's eyes had narrowed. 'Is there someone else? There is, isn't there? Now it all makes sense.' He leaned back in his chair. 'You say you don't want the life we have but of course you do. You just don't want it with me.' He had rubbed his face with his hands in an agitated manner.

'This isn't about someone else, Paul,' Grace had said, pushing away the twinge of guilt she felt. 'And this isn't about you and therein lies the problem. You are not hearing what I am saying. And not once have you said that you love me and you don't want to lose me.'

'That goes without saying,' Paul had countered.

'I disagree,' Grace had replied.

Paul had sighed, his irritation with her evident. 'I'm not sure I like this new you. You're not thinking about anyone but yourself. You're being selfish, Grace!'

'Maybe I am and maybe that is what I need to be right now.'

Paul had laughed a hollow laugh. 'We are getting nowhere.' He had glanced out of the window. 'Listen,' he had said. 'It's getting late. I booked a room in a hotel in Bunessan. Let's sleep on things and regroup tomorrow.'

I'm not your employee, Grace had thought but bit her tongue.

'I won't tell you anything else tomorrow, Paul,' Grace had said instead.

'Yeah well, I'll take that chance.' Paul had stood up to leave. 'I want us to make a decision tomorrow, Grace. You are either coming home with me or we are done.'

'That doesn't sound like much of a decision-making process, Paul, it sounds more like blackmail.'

'Whatever, it's your call. That's what you want isn't it?' Paul's tone had taken on a note of sarcasm and without waiting for a reply, he had walked out of the room. 'Don't worry, I'll find my own way out,' he had called before slamming the front door.

Grace focused on her breathing, trying to calm her jangled nerves. Even though the confrontation had been scary, she felt proud of herself for standing her ground. She had communicated clearly, been assertive instead of submissive. That was progress.

But there were also things that didn't sit right with her. Walking out of her life was one thing, being somewhere new, meeting new people like Josie and Tom, but then being confronted with her 'old' life and essentially forced to make a decision, well, somehow she hadn't been prepared for that.

But what had she imagined would happen? That her life would remain there, waiting for her if she chose to return to it? It was highly unlikely and yet Grace had to admit to herself that she hadn't really thought things through. She had made the decision to walk out, yes, but she hadn't thought about things beyond that.

And in a way she had been drifting, following Josie around, becoming a part of her quest rather than finding her own. If what she had told Paul was true, that she needed to find her own path, then she did indeed have some decisions to make beyond whether or not her relationship with Paul would survive. And there was Tom to consider too. Things had seemed so straightforward initially but now everything was messy, tangled, confusing.

Grace tried to imagine the future Paul had talked about and couldn't. The dynamic between them had changed and Paul would struggle to accept that Grace wanted to make changes. He fell in love with the Grace that looked to him to take the lead. He would find it difficult to relinquish control and to let Grace take the reins.

And beyond that Grace was no longer sure whether she was in love with Paul. She still had feelings for him of course but did she still love him?

Tom's smiling face danced across her mind. How did she end up making things more complicated for herself? Grace sighed, feeling irritated with herself. She turned onto her back and stared up at the ceiling, continuing to mull things over.

And what about work? She couldn't stay with Josie indefinitely, otherwise she was just doing what she had always done under a different guise. She needed some sort of income. She could probably get another accounting job quite easily given her qualifications and experience. But was that what she wanted?

If she was really going to make lasting changes, she might as well consider an alternative career. Her parents would be unhappy of course. They liked Paul and had practically seen her marching down the aisle with a child in each arm. But they would get over it, Grace was sure of it. Her parents would want her to be happy, even if that meant that she was happy in a way they would find difficult to understand.

What Grace was really fighting for was to have the

freedom and independence to decide for herself if she wanted marriage and children or whether she wanted something else entirely. Her stomach felt in knots with anxiety and uncertainty. Grace sat up in bed and took some deep breaths. If she wanted to make her own decisions, these feelings were par for the course and she needed to learn how to deal with them or at best, how to tolerate them.

'Right,' she said out loud and reached over to switch on the bedside lamp. Grace opened the drawer and took out a notebook and pen. She opened it to the first page, smoothed down the blank paper, bit her lip and thought for a moment. And then she began to write.

Josephine (Josie) – Now

Josie took the canvas bag that Greta had left her to sort through and heaved it onto the wooden counter. She was on her second cup of strong coffee, having barely slept after her conversation with Owen last night. Josie sighed. She would have preferred to stay hidden under her duvet instead of doing her shift at the bookshop today. She felt agitated, restless, Owen's words bouncing around her mind tirelessly.

Josie started taking the books out of the bag and inspecting them for any sign of damage. Greta had explained that the amount of damage would determine the price. The bookshop received many donations, especially at this time of the year when people did their spring cleaning.

Surprisingly Josie loved working at the bookshop. She had been sceptical at first but Greta was so enthusiastic and encouraging and she enjoyed chatting to the locals, catching up on island life and getting to know them. There was Angus Mackenzie, a cantankerous man in his early seventies who came once a week and grunted a greeting, but whose eyes lit up when he found a book of Celtic poetry. Or Mrs Boyd with her arthritic hands, who 'popped in' every week to 'see if there are any bargains' and had insisted that Josie please call her Maisie because being called by her surname made her feel old.

She had started to get a feel for which of her customers liked to linger and chat and which liked to be left in peace to browse the shelves. Josie realised that she didn't do this with the people who stayed at her house, preferring to keep things professional and mainly offering short stays. Perhaps it was being here, on the island, that slowly allowed her to open herself up again. To Grace, to the locals, perhaps most importantly to herself.

Owen's words sounded loud and clear in her mind and her shoulders slumped as she realised that he was probably right. She had been hiding. It had felt easier to keep people at arm's lengths, to only do what was necessary to pay the bills.

Her heart was broken and she had tried to protect herself from more pain even though the worst had already happened. She had only allowed herself to love Biscuit. Who wouldn't love that dog? She thought of him fondly and decided to take him on a long walk later.

Perhaps it was time for her to stop running, to stop hiding. She wasn't too old yet to make a fresh start, to try new things. Perhaps it was time for her to start living again.

Josie took another sip of coffee and looked out of the big glass window. The sky was dotted with grey clouds and it looked like it might rain. She thought of Grace then, whose recent past had so suddenly collided with her present. She had been running too until she was forced to stop and to make a decision. Maybe it was time for Josie to make a decision too and a plan slowly formed in her mind and without her noticing, her shoulders relaxed. The bell over the door tinkled its welcoming sound and Josie looked up to see Maisie making her way inside.

'It's a wee bit cold out there,' she announced, shaking her head as if she couldn't believe it. Josie smiled.

'Have you got time for a cup of tea today, Maisie?' she asked. 'Greta might even have stashed some biscuits somewhere.'

'Well if you twist my arm, love, I can hardly say no,' Maisie replied and Josie laughed.

Yes, she liked working here. She liked it very much indeed.

Chapter 9

Grace

Paul was staying at the Seaview Hotel, the only hotel in Bunessan. The hotel overlooked the bay and promised its customers a relaxed atmosphere and cosy rooms. Grace didn't think that it was to Paul's taste as he liked expensive five star hotels with modern and sleek lines, but she reasoned he probably wanted to stay somewhere close. There was nothing Paul hated more than inconvenience.

Paul sat in the conservatory of the hotel, a cup of coffee in front of him. He looked relaxed, at ease with himself. Grace envied him this ability for a moment, before remembering that Paul always looked like that, no matter what was going on for him. It was what made him so good at his job. Grace smoothed over her skirt. She didn't know why but it had felt important to make an effort, perhaps to give her an extra confidence boost. She took a deep breath and approached the table.

'Hi, Paul.'

Paul looked up and gave her a half smile, indicating the chair opposite. 'Hi,' he replied. 'You look nice.'

'Thanks.'

'Would you like a coffee or tea?'

'I'm ok, thank you.'

A silence bloomed between them.

Paul cleared his throat. 'Right then, let's not beat around the bush. What have you decided?'

Grace looked at Paul and took a deep breath.

'I'm not coming back with you, Paul.'

Paul's lips compressed into a thin line of displeasure. 'At last, an answer. So the last five years mean nothing to you then?'

'On the contrary, they mean a great deal. But I need to do my own thing now, Paul. Please try to understand. I want to say thank you for everything—'

'Save it,' Paul interrupted. 'You have already wasted enough of my time, Grace,' he said and stood up. 'I'm not going to waste another second. I'm beyond disappointed in you. But I suppose that doesn't matter to you either.' He looked at her for a moment, his eyes cold.

'Goodbye, Grace,' he said and walked out of the conservatory, without a backward glance.

Grace let out a breath and unclenched her fists. Unexpectedly tears pricked behind her eyes. Surprisingly she did feel upset, but then she had just ended a five year relationship. There had been a time in her life when Paul had meant everything to her; he had been her world.

'Here you go, love,' a kind voice said. Grace startled as the waitress, an older woman with warm brown eyes, put down a bell bottomed glass in front of her with an amber liquid in it.

'Oh, but I didn't order anything,' Grace explained, her voice shaky.

'It's brandy, love. You look like you need it,' the woman replied. 'It's on the house.'

Grace said her thanks and gazed at the glass for a moment.

'Well, Grace,' she said to herself, 'here's to new beginnings,' and she knocked back the brandy.

Josephine (Josie) – Now

Josie cast a critical eye over herself in the mirror and smoothed down her dress. It was a black, knee-length affair made out of a cashmere and merino wool blend. The weather, as ever, was unreliable at the best of times and today would be difficult enough without her having to worry about catching a cold. Josie sighed. The woman looking back at her looked tired and yet there seemed to be some sparkle to her eyes, just a sliver to hint that there was more to her than first met the eye.

Josie knew deep down that she was lucky. She had only vague memories of Owen's funeral after the car accident. She had felt numb and had moved through the motions. His parents had been dead and Sean had been living abroad for a few years, Asia or someplace, she couldn't quite remember but he did make it back for the funeral.

The week before she had been picking out a T-shirt she thought Owen might like and then suddenly there she was, looking at caskets and deciding whether to bury the man that she loved in a coffin, confining him to the cold, dark ground.

In the end she had decided to have him cremated. The ceremony had been lovely, or so she was told by the people who attended, friends mainly and some of his colleagues. And before she knew it, the funeral was over, Sean flew home and life carried on as normal.

Except for her. She had been unable to get back to normal. Normal no longer existed. Josie absentmindedly fingered the engagement ring that she wore on a chain around her neck. It had been yet another shock when the police officer gave it to her and told her they had found it at the crash site. Owen had been about to propose. Fate seemed particularly cruel that day.

And now here she was, getting ready to say goodbye for the second time. This time she would do it properly, not sleepwalking through the motions. Josie knew she had been given a gift. She had been given the opportunity to talk to Owen one more time, something that millions of grieving people never get to do. She had been able to tell him how much she loved him, how sorry she was that she had not been back to Mull sooner.

Somehow the strength she was so renowned for had deserted her when she had needed it the most. The fact that Owen had hung around here, abandoned, made her feel guilty, futile though it was. She couldn't change it. And yet she felt annoyed with herself. In her own suffering she had, albeit unknowingly, added to his.

They say that ghosts stay around the living because they have unfinished business. And if that was true then perhaps Owen's unfinished business was telling her the truth, no bells, no whistles. Perhaps she had always known the truth, deep down, in the darkest corners of her soul. But she saw now that in all the years she had hidden herself away, far away from this island, that she had not been ready to acknowledge the way grief had changed her. The way it had made her feel afraid and incredibly alone.

The irony was that there were plenty of people on Mull that would have supported her, shared in her grief because they too loved Owen. Not only had she done a disservice to herself but also to their friends. Owen had always known how to tell her things she didn't want to hear.

Josie stared at her image in the mirror, her thoughts turning to the idea she had been working on, bringing a smile to her lips.

'Let's do this, Owen,' she said, her voice strong and even. 'Let's get you some well-earned peace.'

Grace

It was a stormy day with rain clouds hanging low in the sky and the wind ripping through the trees. Grace parked the car alongside many others in the car park and helped Josie out of the car.

'How are you feeling?' she asked, knowing it was a rhetorical question. How would Josie feel, finally letting go of the ashes of the man she loved? Probably not great. It was a no-brainer.

'I'm ok, sweetheart,' Josie smiled at her. 'It's time, and more importantly it feels right, in here.' Josie pointed to her heart. Grace nodded and took Josie's arm as they braced themselves against the wind and made their way down the sandy path to the beach.

Josie had issued an open invitation and it looked like most of the village was in attendance. Even after all this time people still remembered Owen and wanted to pay their respects. Although Grace suspected that some of them were mainly here to support Josie, Johnny for one.

'You scrub up well,' she told him as he made his way towards them.

'What? This old thing?' he replied, smiling and smoothing down the crumpled suit self-consciously. 'I thought it best to send off my old pal in style.'

'You look good, Johnny,' Josie said. 'Thank you for being here. Owen is—' her voice broke slightly and she took a breath, 'I mean he would appreciate it,' she finished. Grace squeezed her hand.

'I'm sure he would, but listen, Josie, I'm your friend too and there is nowhere I'd rather be right now. Anything you need, remember?'

Josie smiled at him and patted his arm, tightening her arm around the ashes.

'Grace,' Tom called as he made his way down the path. Despite herself Grace's heart gave a little skip.

'Hi,' she said, brushing the hair out of her face. They hugged, somewhat awkwardly.

'Thanks for coming,' she said, not knowing what else to say.

'Of course,' Tom said. 'I know this probably isn't the place but how have you been? We haven't really talked since, you know—' he broke off.

Grace blushed. Since they slept together. Even though it had only been a few days, it seemed like a lifetime ago to

Grace. So much had happened in between, her unexpected confrontation and break up with Paul, making decisions about her future and today Owen's memorial.

After the break up, she had felt like she needed some time to process what had happened and to say goodbye to the last five years of her life. It had felt important and Grace had realised that lately she was trusting her own instincts more and more. It had made her smile because it meant that she was making progress.

Tom was looking at her. She knew she owed him some answers.

'You're right,' she said, 'this isn't really the time, but maybe afterwards we could talk?'

Tom nodded. 'Sounds like a plan.'

She smiled at him gratefully, relieved he wasn't holding a grudge. Everything with Tom seemed easy. He was a straightforward kind of guy, no games, no pretence. Grace found that she liked it.

She liked it a lot.

Another new thing to add to her list of things she was learning about herself.

'Everyone,' Johnny shouted to be heard over the wind, 'gather round, we are starting.'

Tom followed Grace, who placed herself next to Josie as the rest of the congregation gathered around them in a semi-circle. Grace squeezed Josie's hand and the older woman squeezed back before clearing her voice.

'Thank you, everyone, for coming today,' she began. 'I guess today has been a long time coming. As I'm sure most of you are aware, it has taken me longer than it should have done to make the journey back here, to this island and to the house that was meant to be a home to me and Owen. I can only apologise that it has taken me so long. I guess I was afraid, afraid to say goodbye to the one person who meant more to me than I can ever express in words.'

Josie broke off, taking a moment to collect herself. Grace found that tears pricked her eyes and she blinked them back, surprised. She didn't even know Owen! But she knew how much he had meant to Josie.

'Owen used to say we write our own rules and make our own adventures,' Josie continued. 'That car accident took him from us too early. I felt angry about that for the longest time. I have only recently realised that who he was shines brightly in my memories of him and in my heart and that even though he is no longer by my side, he wouldn't want me to continue feeling all this anger or regret. So today we have come here to say goodbye to Owen, to lay him to rest and to wish him peace. In his memory I wondered if each and every one of you might want to make a promise as we scatter his ashes. A promise to live, to truly live, to maybe change something in your life that is making you unhappy or to do something that you have always wanted to do but keep putting off.'

Josie took a moment to look at the people gathered around her before prising open the lid of the urn.

Slowly she walked towards the ocean, lifted the urn up high and turned it upside down. Owen's ashes got picked up by the wind and carried out to sea in a cloud of grey, like a beautiful bird, towards the horizon.

Free.

Grace closed her eyes and made her promise.

Josephine (Josie) – Now

Josie clutched the now-empty urn in her hands and stared after Owen's ashes as they were picked up by the wind and carried over the sea.

Goodbye, my love, she thought. She had expected to feel heartbroken, wracked again by grief so dense that it swallowed you whole, but to her surprise, a new feeling was sweeping over her, one of relief, a feathery lightness that she hadn't felt in a very long time.

Hope.

Josie turned back to the group and felt comforted by the friendly faces that looked back at her. Grace, Tom and Johnny for one but also Rhiannon, Betty's granddaughter who had taken over the café, Greta and Maisie and even Mr Mackenzie was here, giving Josie a brief nod, which made her smile. This was what she had been missing in her self-inflicted isolation. Community, friendship, a sense of not being on your own because people here looked out for each other.

Josie had asked everyone to make a promise as they remembered Owen. The idea had come to her last night and she felt it to be a fitting tribute to the man she would always love. Her journey to this point had been a long and difficult one but she was here nevertheless. Perhaps pain was still life's greatest teacher. After years of feeling numb and grief stricken, of running and hiding, of sleepless nights and racing thoughts, Josie felt a stillness in her soul that felt calming and restful.

As she had let go of Owen's ashes, she had made a promise of her own.

Owen

It was a stormy day in April, the kind that whips the hair out of your face and leaves you feeling slightly winded, barely able to breathe.

Rain clouds hung low in the sky ready to burst, blocking out the weak sun and giving the air a distinct chill. It wasn't an unusual day for the time of year and yet it was unlike any other day.

It was unique, distinguished from the rest and it would always stand out as such in the years that followed.

That stormy, rainy, chilly day in April was the day I finally broke free.

It was the day I finally found my peace.

Grace

Grace and Tom were walking along the beach. The wind was still blowing, twirling the sand up in front of them but the rain had held off and Grace did not want to be confined to a room. She wanted to be able to talk to Tom, freely and in private without being overheard.

Josie and the rest of the congregation had made their way back to the Black Cow Pub where Johnny had laid on a feast in remembrance of Owen. Grace could imagine that it might be good for Josie to be surrounded by people with whom she could reminisce about Owen. It would surely provide some comfort.

Grace was amazed how well Josie had coped with today.

She had prepared herself for Josie to be frail and devastated but it was almost as if a great weight had been lifted and Josie's voice had been firm and her eyes, whilst teary, had been twinkling and determined.

When Grace had asked her if she was ok, Josie had merely replied, 'He is at peace now,' and smiled. Grace was beginning to realise that Josie was at heart a force to be reckoned with and she smiled a small smile, thinking about the plans Josie had told her about. Perhaps scattering Owen's ashes, whilst being an ending, was also a new beginning for Josie. She certainly hoped so. Josie so deserved to be happy.

Tom cleared his throat beside her, interrupting her thoughts.

'So,' he said, 'you said you wanted to talk?'

Grace couldn't help but laugh.

'You don't beat around the bush do you?'

Tom gave her a sheepish grin.

'Would you care for some mindless small talk first?' he joked.

Grace bumped her shoulder into his in a playful manner and they laughed.

'Paul, my boyfriend, well ex-boyfriend now, came to see me,' Grace began.

'Ah, that explains the radio silence,' Tom said.

Grace blushed.

'I'm sorry I haven't been in touch, Tom. I just, I don't know, needed some time.'

'That's ok,' Tom replied, his eyes finding hers. 'Sounds complicated though.'

Grace nodded.

'When I told you that time in the car that I had to tell you something, well this was it. I was still in the relationship and it didn't feel right somehow to start something else.'

'How long were you together?'

'Five years.'

Tom gave a low whistle.

'Wow, that sounds like a serious relationship.'

'It was,' Grace admitted.

'And now?' Tom asked.

'I ended it, four days ago.'

'I hope you didn't do that because of me. Look, I get it, Grace, you and I, we clicked and we have a good time together, but I don't expect anything from you.' Tom paused for a moment.

'I'm ok if this,' he gestured at them both, 'is just a holiday romance. Although I have to admit that it would break my heart a little bit. I do really like you. Sorry!' He smiled. 'Actually, scrap that, I'm not sorry at all.'

Grace laughed.

'I really like you too, Tom,' she said.

They walked on in silence.

'I didn't break up with Paul because of you,' Grace said after a while. 'I broke up with him because of me. Things between us didn't feel right anymore.'

'Ok. You know, you don't owe me any explanations.'

'I know.'

They smiled at each other.

'So, now that you and Paul are history, there's nothing stopping us from going on a few more dates, is there? Maybe seeing where things take us? No pressure or anything.'

Tom's voice sounded hopeful.

Grace stopped and pulled Tom towards her, kissing him, long and deep.

'What's that for?' Tom asked, smiling against her lips as they came up for air.

'Just because you're one of a kind,' Grace replied, pulling away and carrying on walking, the sand crunching beneath her boots.

'I'm not staying,' she said after a while.

'Wait, what?' Tom asked, stopping, staring at her. 'But you just said you ended your relationship and that you like me.'

Grace forced herself to look at him.

'I do like you, Tom, but I can't stay.'

'Why not?'

'Because I came here to support Josie to do what she needed to do. And now that I've done that, I have to go and do what I need to do for me. I need to figure out what I want, what I want my life to look like, what is important to me. And I can only do that on my own. My whole life I've been dancing to someone else's tune, doing what others thought was best for me. I feel like now I need to dance to my own song, hell, I need to find it first.'

Tom stared at her, stunned.

'Does that make sense? Do you understand what I'm saying?' Grace asked. 'It doesn't mean I don't like you. It's the opposite in fact. If I stay now—' she broke off, unable to complete her thought.

Tom let out a breath.

'I don't know what to say.'

She reached for his hand and squeezed it.

'I get what you're saying, Grace, but I'm wondering what happened?' Tom looked at her, his eyes searching hers. 'What happened to make you suddenly change everything, to turn your life upside down, to question everything?'

Grace felt like she had been punched in the stomach and for a moment she felt like she couldn't breathe.

She closed her eyes for a moment and took a breath.

It was ok.

She was ok.

And this was Tom she was talking to. No one else would need to know. He was still holding her hand and she squeezed it now, concentrating on his warm fingers entangled with hers.

He squeezed back.

Grace took the plunge.

'I tried to kill myself.'

Instead of saying anything, Tom pulled her into an embrace and hugged her tightly. Grace exhaled slowly, the tension leaving her body, tears pricking her eyes.

'You don't have to tell me,' he whispered against her hair.

'I know, but I want to.'

The words had left Grace's mouth before she had time to think about them, but she realised they were true.

And so Grace began to talk.

*

It had been an ordinary Thursday, much like any other.

Grace had had a bad day at the office, a meeting that had gone wrong, a colleague who had ridiculed her and everyone had laughed, including herself, about how she was hopeless at making decisions quickly rather than double checking that she had all the correct information needed and weighing up options.

After her colleagues had dispersed back to their desks, she had gone to the toilet, dabbing at her eyes with a tissue, looking at her flushed face reflected back at her in the mirror. How many days did she mop up tears of humiliation in the office toilets?

'You need to grow a thicker skin, Grace,' Paul had told her on the few occasions she had mentioned being unhappy at work. 'Besides, they're not entirely wrong, are they?' he had added and she had felt her stomach drop. So she was hopeless. The thought had lodged itself firmly inside her head. She had been quiet before but now she practically wished she could be invisible.

When she got home, Paul had messaged her to say that he needed to pull an all-nighter at the office as they were trying to win a big contract and needed to fine tune last-minute details. The house had been silent, unwelcoming and suddenly Grace had been overcome by a feeling of utter loneliness and despair.

She suddenly realised that she was desperately unhappy and had been for quite some time and that realisation settled heavily upon her.

How could she possibly change things?

And why wasn't she happy?

She had everything.

Everyone kept telling her so. She should be grateful. And besides, she was hopeless. She couldn't make changes even if she wanted to.

Where would she even start?

Suddenly life had seemed impossible. The thought of more days ahead like the one she just had made her feel sick and panicky. Grace had opened a bottle of wine and gulped down two glasses in quick succession without really tasting them. She hadn't eaten since breakfast but her stomach felt in knots.

She hadn't realised it then but she had reached breaking point.

A slow build-up of years and years of things that niggled, that didn't quite make sense, suddenly bloomed into a giant knot of anxiety, fear and panic.

And Grace had crumbled as breathtaking sadness swooped over and engulfed her. She had felt breathless, overwhelmed. She kept thinking that she couldn't stand feeling this way. She felt on edge and hopeless. She didn't know what to do or how to help herself.

She just wanted it to stop. The pain, the anxiety, the sadness.

I can't do this anymore, she thought, tears streaming down her face.

You don't have to, her mind had whispered back.

It had been like a lightbulb moment. She could end her suffering. Everyone would be better off without her. No one would really miss her.

The more she thought about it, the more it had made sense.

Grace had found herself in the bathroom in front of the bathroom cabinet, not quite sure how she got there. It was like something had taken over. Her frantic mind felt suddenly calm.

She started popping pills out of their packets. Paracetamol.

Ibuprofen. Some pain medication Paul had been prescribed for a back injury. She found a packet of out of date sleeping pills. The sound of the pills slipping from their packets had felt calming. She had looked at them in the palm of her hand, their different shapes and sizes gazing up at her.

The answer to all her problems.

She started filling a glass with water and slowly, methodically started swallowing the pills. She had crawled into bed, tears flowing unchecked down her face, waiting for death.

For eternal oblivion.

For the pain to end.

And then a thought crossed Grace's mind. Paul would be the one to find her. He would come home from work tomorrow and find her, dead, in their bed. Could she really do this to him? Even though she was convinced his life would be happier without her, how would he cope with the trauma of finding her dead body?

It was like a switch had been flicked.

Grace sat bolt upright, blood rushing to her head.

What was she thinking?

She didn't want to die! Not like this!

The thoughts exploded in her head. She had struggled to her feet, her head drowsy, her limbs feeling heavy and unresponsive. She had dialled 999.

In hospital, she had her stomach pumped and the emergency doctor had told her that they had reached her just in time. Grace had been assessed by the mental health team and she had been apologetic and contrite. She had begged them not to contact Paul and had told them that she wouldn't hurt herself again. It had been an impulsive decision, the result of one bad day too many. The practitioner had held her gaze firmly and eventually agreed, providing that Grace attended therapy and a referral had been made to the local IAPT team. The doctor had kept her in overnight for observation but she was free to leave the following morning.

Grace had gone home, gone to bed and later that afternoon, she had packed her bag and walked out of her life as she knew it.

She had told the doctor that it had been a moment of madness.

What she didn't tell him was that it had actually been a moment of clarity.

*

'I'm so sorry, Grace, it sounds like you've been through a lot!' Tom was still holding her hand, their fingers entwined. As Grace had talked, they had continued walking further down the beach.

'It's ok, Tom,' Grace replied. 'I'm ok.'

Silence settled between them.

'So where will you go?' Tom asked after a little while.

'I have decided to take some time to travel, to see something of the world. I feel like I haven't really been anywhere and I have given it a lot of thought. I just feel like I want to see new places, experience different cultures, find out what I like or don't like, find my own rhythm and pace, you know?'

'Well, they do say travelling blows your mind wide open.'

'Exactly,' Grace said and smiled, pleased that Tom understood her reasoning.

'So you'll be sleeping in hostels and working crappy jobs for a while then,' he joked.

Grace made a face.

'I don't think so,' she said. 'I'm going to do some freelance accounting work, which I can do from anywhere, and believe it or not Josie has asked me to do some accounting work for her. This island is about to have its very own retreat for artists of all kinds. Painters, writers, musicians. Isn't that great?'

Grace beamed at him and Tom returned her dazzling smile.

'Sounds like you've got things pretty much figured out,' he said, and his smile slipped a little.

Grace squeezed his hand.

'I have for the moment.'

They stared at each other, her blue eyes meeting his green ones.

'However,' she said, 'before I leave, I need to tell you about a promise I made.'

Chapter 10

Josephine (Josie) – Now

The sun was streaming through the windows onto the polished floor boards. The cushions on the sofas were plentiful and plumped. The shelves were dust free with books standing to attention, waiting to be picked up and read. The cupboards in the kitchen were stocked with local produce. The beds were made up with fresh linen, the bedrooms carefully prepared, offering just the right combination of luxury and a sense of homeliness.

In the end it had been easy. Once she had made the decision, and throughout the preparations, getting the house cleaned and sorted, hiring someone to set up a website, asking Grace to do the accounts, she wondered again and again what had taken her so long.

What had she been so afraid of?

Loneliness.

Failure.

Not being able to do this without Owen.

But she wasn't doing it without Owen. He was very much part of the whole venture. It would be their legacy. It was always going to be their legacy.

Josie wanted to offer people a haven, to practice their

craft, to free their creativity, to facilitate their journey wherever it might take them. She had always liked being around artists of all kind. Painters, writers, musicians. She admired their ambition and passion, their dedication to a craft that was often misunderstood or romanticised. Being an artist wasn't easy. The hours were long and unpredictable and often recognition was a distant dream. She had known many artists throughout her childhood and later years who had to work in unrelated fields to support themselves.

Josie thought for a moment of her parents. They had instilled in her an appreciation and wonder for the arts. She supposed that had been their legacy. Josie herself had not inherited their musical ability, although she had enjoyed learning the piano as a child, her mother giving her the occasional lesson. Perhaps she would take some piano lessons. The house was certainly big enough for a piano.

Josie glanced into the antique mirror that hung in the entrance hall and straightened her cardigan. She felt Owen's engagement ring dangling right next to her heart. Since the memorial, she had not heard Owen's voice again. She hoped with all of her heart that he was at peace now, finally resting easily.

Somehow the ring didn't weigh as heavy.

She thought about Grace. When Josie had asked her if she would like to do the accounts for the business, she hadn't hesitated. But she had explained that she was not going to stay on the island. She had told Josie that she intended to travel, to see what the world had to offer, to find her own rhythm, her own song.

Josie had felt elated and she hoped that Grace was safe

and happy and finding her own feet. They stayed in touch via emails and video calls and every so often a colourful postcard would find its way onto her doormat. Josie felt like she was vicariously visiting all these places through Grace and she enjoyed it immensely.

Josie had decided to sell her house in England and Holly had been a lifesaver, meeting with estate agents and being her representative. Josie felt that she had come home, that her place was on this island and it hadn't taken her long to become part of the community, what with her work at the Book Shed and popping in at the Black Cow for a cup of tea or sometimes something stronger. In a way it felt like she had always belonged here.

Josie smiled and the woman in the mirror smiled back.

'Ok, Owen,' she said. 'Let's get this show on the road,' and with purposeful movements she opened the front door and walked down the gravelly path to the gate. Once there she turned around the slate sign hanging there to read *Vacancies*. The website had gone live earlier this morning.

She walked back towards the house and took a moment with Biscuit at her side to take in the calm sea and the streak of weak sunlight that suddenly burst through the grey clouds.

The Owen McGregor Artist Retreat was officially open for business.

Epilogue

One year later

It was a cold day, cloudy with a biting wind rushing across the ocean. It was freezing and Grace struggled to keep her footing on the loose sand as she made her way down the hill towards the beach. She shivered and pulled her coat closer around her, holding on to her hat with the other hand.

As she stepped onto the beach, she took a moment and let the scenery sink in. The grey blue of the ocean laid out before her like a rippling table cloth, the vast sky above, the rocky outline of the bay at her back. She marvelled yet again at how beautiful it was here, even on a day like this. The beach lay isolated and remote and for a moment she felt like she was the only person on earth.

Her mind cast back over the last year, how she had ran away only to run away again, before she had found the courage to define life on her terms. She had been to many beautiful places, some remote, some bustling with people and activity. She had swam in oceans, eaten food she never heard of, picked up bits and pieces of languages she never knew existed.

She pushed the sleeve of her coat up to reveal a tattoo on the inside of her wrist. It was of a small anchor with delicate detailing. It was a reminder to herself that there was always hope even if things looked bad.

Grace felt that during the past year her mind had been blown open, her horizons suddenly wide and far stretching. She had allowed herself to be open to opportunities, to try new things and in doing so she had finally found herself, the good and the murkier shades of her being.

There had been times when she felt scared, times when she felt so alone, she could barely breathe. Paul had messaged her several times about the house and in the end, he had paid her out and put all her things in storage, though Grace wasn't sure if she wanted any of them.

They belonged to a different life.

Her parents still remained worried, her father angry at what he saw as her continued defiance, but Grace hoped that they could build bridges in the future. She had grown into her own and it would take time for her parents to get used to this newer, more confident Grace. The therapist Grace had Zoom sessions with was helping her to work through some of these issues.

Whilst Grace had found her sense of self, she had not managed to fully accept herself, but she was working on it. During one of their many phone conversations, Josie had said to her,

'Sweetheart, self-acceptance takes a lifetime and then some. Why do you think I'm as wrinkly as an avocado on a bad day?'

Grace smiled at the memory. Josie truly was one of a kind.

Out of the corner of her eye Grace noticed a movement, breaking her out of her reflections. She turned, noticing a lone figure further along the beach. Slowly, Grace walked towards the person clad in a thick woollen coat, a beanie hat stuck onto cropped hair.

Green eyes locked onto her blue ones, a cheeky smile playing on his lips.

'Hello, stranger,' he said.

'Hello, Tom,' she replied, smiling.

The End

Acknowledgments

Thank you to my family, for always supporting me and for making me laugh.

Thank you, Mama, for instilling a love for reading in me from an early age, which also instilled a love of writing.

Thank you to the Carr family, for all your kindness and love and laughter.

Thank you Rachel for everything.

Thank you to my friends for being there, for listening, for encouraging me and for experiencing the highs and lows with me that life entails.

Thank you, Charlie, for all the cuddles and for cheering me up in the darkest of times.

Thank you, Rob, for having my back, for being the amazing person you are and for introducing me to the beautiful wildness that is the Isle of Mull. I love you.